By ANDREW GREY

Published by DREAMSPINNER PRESS
http://www.dreamspinnerpress.com

Published by DREAMSPINNER PRESS
http://www.dreamspinnerpress.com

Readers Love ANDREW GREY

A Heart Without Borders

"I felt like I was right there with the characters, feeling the heat, the desperation and the total devastation right along with them. There is no doubt in my mind that this book will stay with me for a long time."

—The Novel Approach

"In true Andrew Grey fashion, this book delivers not only a romance but a powerful lesson on the courage, hope and optimism of people in a country devastated by disaster and poverty."

—Hearts on Fire Reviews

Stranded

"*Stranded* is an amazing combination between an intense thriller-like stalker story, a sizzling romance, and a character study which, through tension and drama, brings out the worst and the best in both main characters."

—Rainbow Book Reviews

A Daring Ride

"All the things we've come to love from Grey are there in the print. An emotional, engrossing, and sexy ride is what's in store with this latest work from one of the best authors in the genre."

—MM Good Book Reviews

"I quickly got sucked in by the story and the characters. There really is so much substance in the plot and the people… he doesn't need a lot of extra language to pull you in."

—Mrs. Condit & Friends Read Books

Readers Love ANDREW GREY

An Isolated Range

"Mr. Grey delivers a highly emotional story that captures the reader's heart in one fell swoop... With each range story, you always find yourself drawn in, breathless until the very last page is read."
—Dawn's Reading Nook

"Andrew Grey's Range series just gets stronger with each new book and *An Isolated Range* is perhaps the most amazing addition yet."
—Scattered Thoughts and Rogue Words

"*An Isolated Range* is a story not of human triumphs but also of sadness and death. This is an author who balances both so well that the reader is left speechless after that last page is read."
—Love Romances and More

The Fight Within

"I loved this book, these characters, and this story. Get it today. Read. Understand and through understanding, enjoy."
—Mrs. Condit & Friends Read Books

"This is a story that is rich in detail, delving into the Native American culture and also sharing the suffering that the Native American's still face today."
—MM Good Book Reviews

"This was a very powerful read."
—Live Your Life, Buy the Book

EASTERN COWBOY

ANDREW
GREY

Published by
DREAMSPINNER PRESS

5032 Capital Circle SW, Suite 2, PMB# 279, Tallahassee, FL 32305-7886 USA
http://www.dreamspinnerpress.com/

Eastern Cowboy
© 2015 Andrew Grey.

Cover Art
© 2015 L.C. Chase.
http://www.lcchase.com
Cover content is for illustrative purposes only and any person depicted on the cover is a model.

ISBN: 978-1-63216-704-0
Digital ISBN: 978-1-63216-705-7
Library of Congress Control Number: 2014920685
First Edition March 2015

Printed in the United States of America

This paper meets the requirements of
ANSI/NISO Z39.48-1992 (Permanence of Paper).

To Valerie, Laurel, and my wonderful fans. And to my family for their love and support, even if they are all slightly nuts.

CHAPTER 1

THE PHONE rang, pulling Brighton McKenzie out of the zone. He huffed, wishing he'd remembered to turn the dang thing off. It figured that the brief time his leg decided to behave and let him sit still for more than an hour so he could actually be productive was when people would call. Brighton reached for the phone. He thought about not answering it, but that would mean a message and a voice mail lecture of some kind. It just wasn't worth it.

"Hi, Aunt Vera," he said with what enthusiasm he could muster, which wasn't much.

"I have bad news," she began, but he caught the hint of glee beneath her words. "Your Grandpa Ed passed away yesterday." That explained it. Yes, she was delivering news that was supposed to be sad, so he heard the appropriate tone in her voice, but the excitement was too much for her to keep it at bay completely.

"Yesterday," Brighton said softly. "You could have called." His Grandpa Ed, his paternal grandfather, had been quite old, and his health had been failing, at least according to his dad's sister, Aunt Vera.

"I didn't want to disturb you. It was late. He apparently lay down for a nap and didn't wake up. At least that's what the ambulance people and doctors said. He wanted to be cremated, and we'll spread his ashes at the farm he loved so much after a small memorial service." Now she was really putting on a show. "I'll call you later with all the arrangements."

"Have you called Brianne?" His younger sister.

"I left a message for her to call me back," Aunt Vera answered with barely disguised derision, which meant that she

1

figured Brianne hadn't picked up the phone on purpose for some reason. Their Aunt Vera looked for slights, and she never forgot a single one—real or imagined.

"I'm sure she's busy. She's graduating this weekend." Brighton didn't press it any further. His sister was brilliant, and Brighton was so proud of her he could burst. He'd helped her get her bachelor's degree by working extra jobs, taking side website design projects to pay for it. When she'd gone on to graduate school, Aunt Vera and Uncle Raymond had thought that excessive and said she should get a job. Brighton had told her to follow her own path, which had led her to a fellowship at the University of Maryland. She'd majored in chemistry in college, and even at the undergraduate level she had shown brilliant insight. Now she was getting her master's degree with honors, at the top of her class, and she'd had offers from half a dozen doctoral programs that wanted her badly enough to be willing to pay her tuition and provide her a teaching stipend. She had decided to stay at UM in College Park.

"All that schooling just so she can be better than us," Aunt Vera said.

"She's intelligent, and I want her to go as far as she possibly can." Brianne deserved that. Hell, they both did, but Brighton's life had taken a very different path, and his big dreams had been reduced and changed to just being able to walk and navigate through life without pain or being doped up on pills. "Please call me as soon as you know about the arrangements, and I'll call Brianne and make sure she knows as well."

"Okay," his aunt said. "I have other calls to make, but I'll talk to you soon." She hung up, and Brighton placed his phone facedown on the desk next to him and tried to go back to work. His leg, of course, picked that moment to let him know it ruled his life. Brighton stood, stretching it, and then he grabbed his cane to walk around the living room of his small apartment. The pain and stiffness subsided, and Brighton sat back down, stretched out his leg, and then called his sister.

"What's up?" Brianne said when she answered.

"I don't mean to disturb you. I know you're busy, but our Grandpa passed away yesterday."

Brianne grew quiet. "Is that what Aunt Vera wanted?"

"Yeah," Brighton answered softly. "He went in his sleep, and it seems to have been peaceful."

"That's all any of us can ask for, I guess," Brianne said with a hitch in her voice. "I went out to see him last week, and he seemed just as active and energetic as usual." She paused, and then Brighton heard her blow her nose. "I suppose that's what he would have wanted—to be active up to the last and then go."

"Exactly," Brighton said, his throat closing slightly. "Do you remember him walking us around the yard on the pony?"

"Diablo? Yeah." She chuckled. That pony was as gentle as could be, but for some reason Grandpa had named the poor thing Diablo. Grandpa had a sense of humor, but sometimes he was the only one who got it. "And he sat with you for hours in the hospital after the accident."

"I know. And he held my hand after that last surgery when they thought they might have to take my leg altogether. He yelled at them for being quitters and said that since I wasn't a quitter, they weren't going to be either. I swear they saved my leg because of him."

"Are you still in a lot of pain?" Brianne asked.

"It's lessening. The doctors say they don't understand why, but it is. I just have to remember not to sit for too long at one time." He sighed. "Let's talk about something else. Maybe this weekend if you have a few hours, we can take a ride out to the farm, say good-bye to him in our own way." The words barely made it out of his mouth. Brighton wiped his eyes and swallowed hard.

"Yeah, let's do that." Her voice broke as well. "Graduation is Sunday. We could go out to the farm on Saturday. I still have a key to the house." Brianne paused again. "You know Aunt Vera and Uncle Raymond will sell the place as soon as they possibly can."

"I know," Brighton said. Their aunt and uncle had been waiting for Grandpa Ed to pass away for years. The family farm, which Grandpa had lived on and worked to a small degree, was located in Ellicott City and was now surrounded by condominiums and housing developments. Grandpa hadn't been interested in selling. The farm was his home—the only one he'd ever known. But his daughter, Vera, and her husband saw the place as a gold mine and their ticket to retirement. "Doesn't matter, though. Not really." Brighton swallowed because it did matter; he just couldn't voice it, and it felt… easier for him not to explain. He figured Brianne understood, anyway. "We can't change it."

"No," Brianne said. "Look, I still have to get some work done. I'll call you as soon as I'm finished, and we can make plans for Saturday. Are you planning to come to the graduation ceremony? I'll understand if it's too much sitting for you."

Brighton smiled. "Are you kidding? I'll eat pain pills for hours to see you get this degree. You worked hard for it, and I'm so proud of you."

"I wasn't the only one who worked hard, and don't think I could ever forget all you did for me."

"It's what Mom and Dad would have wanted."

"No. They would have wanted both of us to be getting our master's. They believed in education and the value of knowledge."

"Then I'll watch you get your degree for both of us." He smiled because he was indeed very proud of her. "I'm content and happy in my own way. You're the one with the grand ambitions. I'm pleased enough doing what I like and supporting myself." That had been an accomplishment in itself. He had been afraid after the accident that not only would he never walk again, but he'd be dependent upon others for the rest of his life. And the thought of Aunt Vera taking care of him was too *Baby Jane* for words.

"I know you think you are, but you deserve to be truly happy."

Brighton groaned.

"Come on. You need to get out more and have some fun. Meet some people."

"Look who's talking," Brighton countered. "Maybe if you took your own advice, you'd meet someone, and I could marry you off."

"Ha-ha," she said. "I was thinking more along the lines that I could marry *you* off to some strong, handsome man, and then I wouldn't have to worry about you being alone all the time."

"Yeah. I think I'll go out dancing Saturday night. I'll be a huge hit until I whack someone with my cane or fall flat on my face. I could just stand at the bar and get plastered. That might be nice." Like the guys at any of those clubs would look twice at a guy like him. He'd never been pretty or cute, and with the gimpy leg, well… that really added to his attractiveness… not!

"Quit being a sourpuss. I'm not saying to go out to the clubs. You never did that much—at least not as far as I know. But find a hobby, call your friends, go out for dinner. Anything but sitting around in your living room in your underwear in front of the computer all the time."

Dammit. Brighton looked down and cringed but said nothing. He wasn't going to tell her she was right. He did need to get dressed every once in a while.

"I'll talk to you soon," Brianne said.

"Okay. I'll let you go kick some academic butt." Brighton hung up and stared at his computer screen. He really wasn't interested in going back to work, but he needed to get this job done. Brighton sighed and forced his mind back to the task at hand. He could let the sadness overwhelm him later.

After working for another two hours, he finished up the last detail and sent a note for his customer to take a look at the site. He hoped they would be pleased. Brighton stood, his leg stiff but quiet on the pain front. Forcing his joints to move, he made his way to the bathroom, stripped, and started the shower.

The hot water felt amazing, especially on his leg. Brighton washed and then stood under the water, letting it soothe his knee and hip. Eventually he had to get out, so he turned off the water and carefully stepped out of the shower. The last thing he needed was to fall and hurt himself. He'd done that once and had no intention of doing it again, thank you very much. He dried off and went to his room, where he dressed. He had just finished up and was debating starting a new project when his phone rang again. Brighton wasn't particularly keen to speak with his aunt, but he picked up the phone. The display showed a number he didn't recognize.

"Hello," he said tentatively, expecting some telemarketer. He hated those people.

"Good afternoon, is this Mr. Brighton McKenzie?"

"Yes."

"Excellent. I'm Arthur Granger, and I was your grandfather's attorney. I'm also in possession of his will, and as you're named in it, I'd like to meet with you. Edward was old-fashioned and specified that we read the will to all the beneficiaries after his death. I know it's usually not done that way these days, but it was his wish. Can you and your sister Brianne be available this time tomorrow? I left her a message, but she hasn't returned it."

"She's graduating with her master's degree this weekend, so she's very busy. But I'll check with her and let you know if there's a problem."

"That will be fine," he said and gave Brighton the address and time. "Do you need transportation? Your grandfather said at the time he made the will that you sometimes have trouble getting around. I can have a car sent."

"If she can come, then Brianne will give me a ride." Brighton felt helpless. "Thank you." He remained polite and kept the frustration out of his voice.

"Then I'll see you tomorrow at two." The lawyer disconnected, and Brighton called his sister again. He explained what was happening, and she confirmed that she could be done by noon. She would come by, they could have a quick lunch, and then go to the lawyer's office. Neither of them speculated about what could be in the will for them. There was no need. Neither of them wanted anything from their grandfather other than to have him back in their lives.

THE FOLLOWING afternoon, Wednesday, Brianne rushed into his apartment in Laurel. "I got here as fast as I could."

"I wasn't expecting you for another half hour. Did you get everything done?" Brighton said as he walked over to greet her, leaning on his cane.

"I thought you said things were better?" she said with a glower, her hands on her hips the exact way their mother had done when they were children and she thought she had caught one of them in a lie.

"There's less pain, and I can get around a little better. Don't try that look on me, little sister." He headed for the door. "Let's go eat so we can find out what this nonsense with the lawyer is all about."

They left, and Brianne drove him to a nearby pizza restaurant that had the world's best pizza, made in coal-fired ovens. He loved the stuff, and Brianne humored him. Once they were done, he handed her the piece of paper with the address on it. She programmed it into the GPS, and they were off. It took about twenty minutes to find the lawyer's office, and they arrived and got out of the car as their aunt and uncle did the same.

"You got a call as well?" Aunt Vera said. "That's nice of Daddy to remember the two of you." The smile seemed genuine. She embraced them both, as did their uncle, and then they headed inside.

Aunt Vera took charge, and soon they were all ushered into a rather nice conference room. The lawyer came in with a folder, made introductions, and then motioned for them all to sit.

"I'm bound by Edward McKenzie's wishes in these matters. He asked me to read the will to all of you. With the exception of the legalities, he dictated the will himself, so it's very much in his own words. I'll skip the legal portions and come to the heart of the matter, if you're all agreeable."

They all nodded, and Brighton shifted in the chair, his leg aching. He rubbed it to soothe it.

Mr. Granger opened the file. "The last will and testament of Edward McKenzie," he said ceremoniously and then began to read.

"To start with I'd like to deal with my daughter Vera Westbridge. Vera, honey, I know you and that man you married are counting on the proceeds of the farm for your retirement. Well, I got to tell you, nobody gave me anything. I worked my entire life on that land, and no one is going to use it so they can sit on their butt in Florida or some other place and bake their brains out. It's time you did for yourself, so I'm leaving you fifty thousand dollars. It's not enough to retire on, but that's life. You need to stand on your own two feet, so I'm giving you a shove."

Aunt Vera gasped and looked at Uncle Raymond, her mouth hanging open like a startled fish. She didn't move or breathe for a long time and then burst into tears.

Mr. Granger continued, "There's no use crying. It isn't going to do you no good because there's no one around to hear it who cares. You always turned on the waterworks when you wanted something, and most everyone gave in. Well, now I'm dead, so I don't care how much you cry." It appeared to Brighton that Mr. Granger was getting a little kick out of this, but he was too good a lawyer to say anything or let it show on his face.

"After all I did for him. His own daughter, and he did this to me." She sniffled, and Uncle Raymond did his best to soothe her. However, that didn't last long as the realization of what was about to happen sank in. Her expression darkened, and she glowered at Brianne and Brighton.

"For my granddaughter, Brianne McKenzie. Dear, you never needed anything from anyone. You have a firm head on your shoulders, and I know you'll go far. I leave you fifty thousand dollars to do with as you see fit. I hope you continue with your schooling and change the world." Mr. Granger looked up from where he was reading and smiled at Brianne, who seemed very pleased and excited. That would go a long way to ensuring a good start for her.

Brighton breathed a slight sigh of relief.

"For my other grandchildren, I leave ten thousand dollars each. I'm not specifically naming them, but they include Vera and Raymond's children. Granger will ensure they each get their share. Now to my grandson, Brighton McKenzie. Brighton, I leave you the rest of my estate, including the farm, its contents, and any other money, on the provision that you live there for at least two years, at which point everything is yours. You are free to sell the farm, but if you do so within the first two years, the proceeds will be split evenly among yourself, Brianne, and my daughter Vera." The lawyer paused, and Brighton gasped as the weight of what was happening fell on him. Brighton was so shocked he barely had the ability to draw air. "After your parents were killed by the drunk driver, you stepped up and raised your sister almost on your own. You had help from your aunt and uncle as well as myself, but by and large you did what needed to be done, fighting all of us sometimes to make sure you could do what you thought was right. I know we had some really whooping matches, but I was never mad at you. You stood up to all of us, and that makes you a man. You also put your own life on hold and worked as hard as you could to see to it that Brianne got through school."

Brighton looked to Brianne. He had never talked about what he'd done for her. That had been between them.

"Your grandfather knew a great deal about you," Mr. Granger said. "He was very intelligent and observant, and he seemed to know what was going on within his family."

"So he gets the farm? He can't even walk very well. How is he supposed to take care of it?" Aunt Vera said.

Brighton opened his mouth to argue, but Mr. Granger cleared his throat and returned to the will. "Now I know that my daughter Vera will try to persuade you to simply sell the land so she can get her hands on the money, and you are free to do that if you wish, but it is my hope that you will live on the farm and let it become part of you. That land has been in our family since Colonial times, longer than this country has existed. Listen to your own heart and make up your own mind." Mr. Granger stopped. "The rest of the will contains stipulations should any of the recipients not survive him and so on. They do not pertain to you at this time."

His aunt practically jumped to her feet. "I want a copy of this will so I can have my attorney look at it. Daddy gave me a copy of his will three years ago, and it was nothing like this."

"This will was executed six months ago and was registered with the court at that time. You will, of course, be provided with a copy, and you may have whoever you wish look at it, but there is little you can do to alter any of the provisions. Mr. McKenzie was very specific about his intentions and why he wished to divide his assets the way he did. Nothing more is necessary."

Aunt Vera fumed for a while and then got up to leave, dragging Uncle Raymond behind her. She was obviously furious, and he appeared broken and fit to be tied.

"So what do I do now?" Brighton asked Mr. Granger.

"The will needs to be probated, and then the property will officially revert to you, but in the meantime I suggest you take up residence there and get on with your life. Your grandfather was… anxious that the farm remain in the family. He said his original intention was to leave it to your father."

"But why me?" Brighton asked and turned to Brianne.

"Because someone should do something nice for you," Brianne told him. "You deserve it, and I think Grandpa knew that."

"You're not mad?"

"That Grandpa left you the farm? Hardly. I'm not interested in it, and if you can make something of the farm, more power to you. The money he left will mean I can continue the work on my PhD without interruption."

Wait, he thought everything was all set for her. "What are you saying? I thought…."

"I know what you thought. I lied. You would have moved heaven and earth to make sure I got that degree, but you've done enough for me. I'll stand on my own two feet now as long as you do the same." She smiled and stood before pulling him into a hug. "You'll get no animosity from me, big brother." Brianne looked toward the door. "I wish I could say the same about our other relatives."

"Aunt Vera wants what she wants, and she always pushed the men in her life to get it for her. I guess Grandpa wised up."

"So you'll be keeping the farm?" Mr. Granger asked.

"I don't know what I'm going to do." Brighton slowly got to his feet. "It isn't like I can take care of a farm. I can hardly get around some days, so taking care of even the few animals Grandpa still had will be beyond me." Brighton swallowed hard. "And what am I supposed to do for money? The place is going to take more of it than I have. It needs work."

"Your grandfather specified that you received the remainder of his estate. He left approximately a quarter million in cash after other estimated expenses. After the other bequests, that leaves approximately $130,000. So you will have the cash to maintain the farm should you choose to."

Jesus. He'd had no idea. Brighton leaned on the conference table to steady himself. It was a lot of money, though he knew on a farm that wouldn't last very long. But it would buy him some time and maybe the ability to hire some help, especially if he gave up his apartment and lived in the house so he could save expenses. At least he hoped so. "I have no idea where to begin. I visited Grandpa whenever I could, but I never lived there. I used to feed some of the animals, and when I was younger I rode the pony, but I don't know anything about running a farm." Brighton was beginning to feel a little overwhelmed. "Maybe I better have some time to think about things."

"I think that would be a good idea. And if there's anything you need, please don't hesitate to call." Mr. Granger gathered his papers into the file folder, stood, and got ready to leave the room. "I understand this is a big decision, and I have to admit that I didn't know your grandfather very well. My father was his attorney for years, and after he passed away, I took over. I met with your grandfather just a few times to update his will. But I can say that he impressed me as a man who knew his own mind and cared deeply about both of you. He also…." Mr. Granger paused. "I use words for a living, but I'm having trouble explaining what I want to say. Your grandfather loved that land. It was a part of him as much as his arms and legs. He knew his daughter would sell. He said she was never happy there, even as a child."

"What are you saying?" Brighton asked.

"That your grandfather left you the farm for a reason. He didn't confide in me what that reason was. But it's more than just keeping it in the family, I feel that. Maybe he said something to you at some point."

Brighton tried to think if there was anything. He shook his head. "Thank you."

"You're very welcome." Mr. Granger waited for them to leave the conference room and escorted them out to the lobby area. "I suspect you're going to need some help."

"Yes." Brighton looked down at his bad leg. "I can stand for an hour at most, and sitting in one place for any length of time is painful. So there isn't much I can do at the farm." He was downright helpless when it came to anything physical. His balance was poor as well, which only added to his fear of falling.

"I have this cousin," Mr. Granger began. "He's from the wild side… well, let me just say that the family hasn't had a lot to do with him over the past few years. He left home when he was eighteen and roamed around the country. The last place we know he worked is some ranch in Montana. He doesn't talk much. Never has." He leaned closer and lowered his voice. "People used to think he was slow, but I think he's just quiet and maybe a little shy. He needs a job, and I could see if he's interested in helping you out with the farm. He's not a stranger to hard work, and he has done ranch work, so he understands that kind of thing." He seemed uncomfortable. "You don't need to feel obligated to hire him in any way, of course. I haven't spent any time around Tanner in a long time. But it wouldn't hurt for you to talk to him."

Brighton nodded. "Send him by or have him give me a call. I'm not sure what I'm going to need, but help is a definite." He shook Mr. Granger's hand and then followed Brianne out of the office and to the car.

"Where do you want to go?" she asked, sitting in the driver's seat without starting the engine.

"Home to hide," Brighton answered honestly. "But since you're here, let's go out to the farm and have a look around." He got as comfortable as he could and fastened his seat belt. Brianne started the engine, and the air-conditioning began to banish the sauna feel from the car. "What are you going to do with the money?"

"What Grandpa said."

Brighton turned toward her. "What's all this about needing money and not telling me?"

"I don't need money. But I exaggerated the fellowship benefits just a little. They'll pay for most things, like the classes and the dissertation credits, but the stipend isn't enough to live on, even if I exist entirely on ramen. So the money will make sure I can complete the degree in the next three or so years. I don't want to take forever." They pulled to a stop at a light. "I know you'd make sure I had what I needed, and you'd pay for it without thinking about it. But I don't want you to. It's time you had a life of your own, and you can't do that if you're still supporting me. I need to be on my own, and you need to let me." The light turned green, and they moved forward.

"I do have my own life."

"You sit home, work, watch television, work, talk to me on the phone, work, sleep, go nowhere, work, baby your knee and leg, work…. I think you're getting my point."

"I work," he grumbled.

"You work hard, and you've used all that you've earned for me. From now on I'll take care of me, and you can get a life. You're a landowner now. There will be people beating a path to your door."

"Please, you make it sound like we live in Elizabethan England."

"You just need to make the land pay. And it can. The land is good—it always has been—and I don't think Grandpa did much with it lately, so it's been sitting, which is good for replenishment. You just need to figure it out."

"It would be easier to sell it," Brighton said, looking out the window at the passing houses and shopping centers.

"Don't you dare," Brianne scolded sharply. "Yes, Aunt Vera and Uncle Raymond took us in after Mama and Daddy were killed, but they did it out of obligation, and they never let either of us forget it. They treated Mick, Tim, and Jill as though they were royalty and us as though we were the bastard stepchildren." Brighton gasped softly. "Don't sound so surprised. I know you took the worst of their anger and resentment to try to shield me from it. But I have eyes, and I'm not dumb." She slowed and made the last turn. "You're an amazing big brother, and I want you to do what will make you happy."

"Thanks." Brighton didn't know what else to say. "I think I'm a little overwhelmed."

Brianne slowed the car at the farm and turned into the familiar drive, then pulled up to the house. "What's going on?"

Aunt Vera's car was parked beside the house. "Pull right up behind them," Brighton said.

Brianne turned to him with one of her evil grins. She did as he asked, stopping within an inch of their bumper. Aunt Vera and Uncle Raymond weren't going anywhere unless they tried to drive over them or went right through the garage. Brighton got out, and Brianne did the same. They looked up as Aunt Vera and Uncle Raymond came around the corner, each carrying a box.

"I suggest you turn around and put that back," Brianne snapped.

"But these are things Daddy wanted me to have," Aunt Vera began.

"If he did, they would have been in the will. The farm and all the contents were left to Brighton." She stormed up to them already under a full head of steam. "That's all Brighton's, and I know my brother—if you had asked, he would have thought about it and probably given you what you wanted, but as it is I think you've blown that chance."

Aunt Vera lifted the box, and Brighton could see she was getting ready to drop it. "We'll see about that," she said.

"Don't you dare," Brianne threatened and stepped forward. She snatched the box, turned around, and shoved it at Brighton. He dropped his cane and managed to stay on his feet as he took it.

"After all we did for you!" Uncle Raymond sputtered. There were many times when Brighton wondered if he could speak at all. It turned out he just rarely got a word in edgewise.

"Like what?" Brianne said. "We were kids who had lost our parents, and you treated us as an obligation. We needed support, understanding, and care, but what we got was demands and sarcasm. Or else you ignored us. You made us feel unwelcome the entire time we lived with you, and during that time what there was of our parents' estate—"

"We used that to benefit you," Aunt Vera said.

"No, you used it to take trips to Disney World and deigned to take the two of us along. I know what you did and how you made us feel, but all that's over. Now, you will turn around and put everything back, including what you already have in the car, or I'll call the police and have you both arrested for theft. Brighton's too nice, but I'm not." She glowered at them and took the box from Uncle Raymond, placing it on the ground near the house. Then she took the box from Brighton, who breathed a sigh of relief because he was seconds from either dropping it or losing his balance. She retrieved his cane and handed it to him. "Go on inside. I'll take care of these two."

"There's nothing in our car," Aunt Vera said, but Brighton barely paid attention to her. Brianne had a good head of steam, and he'd let her deal with it. She obviously had plenty of resentment, and she could vent it all at them if she wanted. Brighton wasn't going to stop her.

"You aren't leaving until I see for sure, and that means emptying your suitcase-sized purse," Brianne said as Brighton stepped up onto the porch and then over to the open front door. He didn't step inside right away. Instead, he took a few seconds to glance around. The rocking chair that was old as the hills still sat in its usual place on the porch. Grandpa had spent many an hour smoking his pipe in that chair. Apparently Grandma hadn't let him smoke in the house, and even after she died, he still sat in his rocking chair to have his pipe. Brighton lowered himself into the chair and placed his hands on the arms. Voices reached his ears, but he ignored them as he rocked slowly back and forth. The wooden chair should have felt uncomfortable, but it didn't. It felt like it fit him, and as the perpetually tense muscles in his leg relaxed, Brighton sighed.

Eventually Brianne backed her car up the drive and parked off to the side. Then their aunt and uncle's car turned around in the yard and pulled defiantly down the drive. Brighton knew he was projecting their attitude onto the car, but it was how it looked. "You pissed them off good," he said as Brianne stepped onto the porch with one of the boxes.

"Do you know what she had in her purse? All of Grandma's jewelry. The things Grandpa gave her over the years. And then the boxes...."

"I figured when I saw that they'd come here right from the lawyers. If we'd been ten minutes later, they would have been gone."

"That's exactly what they were doing," Brianne said, carrying the box inside. She went out to the driveway again and then came up the porch steps with the other box and carried it inside before returning. "They also took the vases Dad gave Grandma that he bought on his trip to England years ago."

"The Wedgwood ones?" Brighton asked.

"That's what the old battle-ax was going to smash. If she couldn't have it, no one could. Well, I'm tempted to—"

"Just let it go. They aren't going to try anything more. They were whipped good and sent packing. I doubt they'll ever show up here again."

"But...."

"They'll turn the rest of the family against us, but who gives a damn. We haven't seen any of the distant relatives in years." Brighton closed his eyes.

"Do you want to go inside?"

"No. I'm going to sit here for a while. You go ahead, and take whatever you want." He wasn't going to deny her anything.

"There are a few things I'd like. I'll put them on the table so you know, and you can give your permission." She went into the house and quietly closed the door, leaving him alone with the wind and his memories of his grandfather.

BRIGHTON LOST track of the amount of time he sat in his grandfather's rocking chair. It was warm enough, and the breeze felt perfect. But after a while the sounds and activity intruded. He stood up and used his cane to steady himself as he walked to the edge of the porch. Off to the west, a huge condominium complex stretched as far as the eye could see: light blue aluminum-sided buildings with white trim that seemed to go on forever. On the other side, a shopping center rose at the edge of his grandfather's land—now his land. And he knew that behind the house was a subdivision of one- and two-family homes crammed together on postage stamps of land. Sure, he knew he could get a lot of money for the land, possibly millions, but this was an oasis of green in a forest of tacky modern homes.

"You're up," Brianne said.

"Just thinking," Brighton said without turning around.

"The house is decent and very well built, that's for sure, but it needs to be updated. Badly. The kitchen is the one Grandma used, and nothing has been changed. There are things you're going to need to do and fast. The electrical service is old and will need to be replaced, and there isn't any air-conditioning. I went down into the basement, and it's clean as a whistle, but I saw the electric box. I think Thomas Edison invented it along with his lightbulb."

"How do you know stuff like that?" Brighton sure as hell didn't.

"I read a lot, and I'm a science geek. I love stuff like electricity, magnetics, and how things work. You should know that."

"I guess." Brighton laughed. "I remember when Mom and Dad got you a battery-operated Barbie car. You played with it for a few years and then took it apart to see how it worked." Brighton turned around. "Do you think it's safe to live in?"

"Of course. You just need to call an electrician and have some work done. Everything is doable, and you're going to want air-conditioning. How Grandpa lived without it is beyond me, but you're going to have to have it, especially since window units might start blowing fuses. There's a whole box of them in the basement."

Brighton nodded. "Let's look around." He turned and went inside. The place looked just as he expected and remembered. The living room had the same sofa and chairs it had always had. It was like stepping into a time capsule locked away for fifty years.

"I checked the upstairs, and there's going to need to be a lot of cleaning. Everything is covered in dust. It doesn't seem like it's in bad condition or anything, just neglected."

"Well, it isn't going to get less neglected with only me here." Stairs were a problem for Brighton. Especially full flights—he hated the things. But then again, maybe it was time for him to figure out how to navigate them and move forward.

"There are some big bedrooms and a huge bath. Clean things up, and you'll love it." Brianne grinned. "The bathroom is heaven. It's old, but dang, the room is really big. There's space for an army. I'm almost jealous. I remembered it being big as a kid, but sometimes memories get distorted."

He wandered through the main floor, then stopped at the foot of the stairs and peered upward. "I wonder if there are still animals. They'll need to be fed and watered if there are. Lord knows our aunt and uncle would let them starve in their rush to sell." He turned away from the imposing stairs. He could figure that out later.

"I'll go check. But I'm not cleaning any stalls. I didn't dress this morning for farm work."

Brighton hadn't either. Hell, he'd figured he might get a small inheritance and that was it. "I'll go with you. Together we can probably keep anything from starving to death." He hoped. Brighton walked slowly, closing the front door behind them. Brianne strode across the yard to the small barn and pulled open the door. Brighton stepped inside. Animals bleated and baaed. A pony lifted its head, staring at him with doleful eyes. He peered over the stall wall and saw an empty manger and water trough. "Fuck," Brighton swore and looked around. He found a bale of hay and managed to get the twine undone and drop some hay in the manger. "Is there a bucket?"

"I found one back here. Nothing has water, and most all the mangers are empty," Brianne called back as she pulled open a door. "There's feed in here. Thank God it's labeled. I don't know how much to give, but we can do our best."

"I'll handle the feed if you'll get the water. Start with the pony."

Brianne agreed and began hauling buckets of water from the tap just inside the barn. Neither of them could find a hose, so Brighton added that to his growing mental list of things to get. He also added another item to the "things that scare the shit out of me" list as well as the "how the fuck am I supposed to do this on my own" list. How his grandfather had watered the animals was beyond him, but he always was stubborn, and things had to be done his way.

One-handed, he got feed to the four goats and four sheep. Brianne made sure they all had water. "We might as well let them out into their pens if we're going to be here a while." She opened doors, and after a while the animals wandered outside into their enclosures. Then she joined Brighton in the center of the barn. "I can come over for a few days to help with cleaning and make sure the animals are fed. But this place needs more help than I can give."

"I know," Brighton sighed. "I keep thinking I should just sell and give everyone their money. I hate to do it, but I can't take care of a place like this. I manage to take care of myself, and that's about it." This was overwhelming in the extreme.

"Breathe, big brother, and take it one step at a time. There aren't so many animals that it's a huge job. There are nine total." She rolled her eyes. "There aren't herds of goats and flocks of sheep. Get on the Internet, find out how to care for them, get a hose, buy feed, and go at it. It will be good for you to care for something other than just yourself."

Brighton could feel his chest pounding and gasped for air. He closed his eyes and pushed away the panic that started to rise. "It's too much."

"It is not!" she told him firmly. "Now get over it, and stop feeling sorry for yourself. You were given a gift today, so don't squander it." She placed her hands on her hips and glared at him. "Where is the man who stood up to Aunt Vera when we were kids and told her to go to hell when she said she didn't think I should go to college? As I remember, you told her that I was going to college because 'I was going to make more of myself than a stupid cow like her.'" Brianne grinned. "You had spunk and confidence."

"That went away a long time ago."

"Well, get it back, because the mousy Brighton is starting to get on my nerves." In that moment she sounded just like their mother.

"Rather than concentrating on what you think you can't do, figure out what you can. The rest you can find people to help you with." Brianne stepped out of the barn and into the sunshine. "This is a small piece of heaven in the midst of suburban sprawl. Or it could be. This could be your piece of heaven. You don't have to do what Grandpa might have done or listen to anyone else. Make it yours."

"How in the hell did you get to be so smart? I'm the big brother. It's my job to give you advice."

Brianne scoffed and smiled at him. "Please. I was always the smart one, and you know it." She put her arm around his shoulder. "Now let's go in the house and see what's good for now and what needs to be done." Brighton nodded and followed Brianne back into the house. "I'm going downstairs to get a bucket I saw." She left, and Brighton heard her on the stairs. She returned with buckets that she'd filled with every cleaner she seemed to be able to find. Then she hauled dusters, brooms, and the cleaning gear upstairs.

Brighton pulled out his phone and the card from the lawyer. He called the number and asked to speak to Mr. Granger. After a few seconds, his call was answered. "Mr. Granger, I think I'm going to need some help."

"Please call me Arthur, and I'll do what I can."

Brighton explained about the visit from his aunt and uncle.

Arthur was none too pleased. "We'll use that to our advantage if they start causing trouble."

"Good. Brianne and I are at the farm, and it's evident that I won't be able do this on my own. The animals didn't have food or water when we got here."

"I was told by your aunt that they would take care of them."

"Well, I doubt they did that. There was nothing left at all. Anyway, we got the animals sorted, and they're going to be fine. If your cousin would be interested, he's welcome to stop by the farm tomorrow afternoon, and we'll talk."

"Very good. But I want to stress you aren't under any obligation. If you don't want to hire him, I'll understand."

"I appreciate that. Thank you. We'll talk and then see what we both think." That was all Brighton could promise, but he was a little desperate.

"Fair enough." Arthur paused, and Brighton heard papers rattling. "Your aunt called a while ago. Apparently she's still interested in making the funeral arrangements. Your grandfather has been cremated already, and his wish was to have his ashes scattered at the farm."

"Brianne and I will do that after the service."

"She said she had to move the memorial service to Sunday."

Brighton swore under his breath. "It needs to be on Saturday. Sunday Brianne is receiving her degree, and she isn't going to miss that. Aunt Vera is being mean." Brighton took a deep breath. "I'm assuming from what you said that you are acting as executor."

"Yes."

"Good. Then go ahead and lay down the law with her. We already had the pleasure of doing that today. I guess it's your turn." Brighton smiled.

"I didn't want to cause any undue family strife."

"Too late for that," Brighton quipped.

"I'll handle everything from this end."

"Thank you." This was ridiculous, and he wasn't going to put up with Aunt Vera being a pain. How could she do this to her own father? Let him rest in peace, and let the family say good-bye. "I appreciate all the help. I just can't deal with my aunt's pettiness right now. I could sic Brianne on her, but we might end up with a double funeral and then a murder trial."

Arthur chuckled. "I'll handle it."

"Thank you," Brighton said. He hated putting him in the middle of a family fight, but his aunt was being vindictive, and he didn't have the energy to fight with her right now.

"Were you on the phone?" Brianne called down from upstairs.

"Yes. The attorney is going to send his cousin over tomorrow. Don't know if he can help or will be interested, but I have to try." Brighton paused while he decided what to tell her. "Vera is up to her tricks. She said that she needed to move the memorial service to Sunday."

"That witch!"

"Don't worry. I sicced the attorney on her. He'll take care of it. She had already made arrangements and things, so the old bat is just being mean."

Brighton's leg began to shake, so he went back outside and sat in the chair on the porch. He should go upstairs and try to help Brianne, but the ache in his leg said he'd done what he could do for today. "I hate this," he said out loud. The truth was, he felt useless most of the time. He could work and was good at what he did, but functioning in the real world was a pain in the ass. He couldn't drive. He didn't have enough muscle control in his right leg to depress the accelerator and brake pedal with any degree of finesse. For three months he'd kept hoping his leg would improve. The doctors said it would, but it hadn't happened yet.

His phone rang, and Brighton answered it even though he didn't recognize the number.

"Hello, is this Brighton?" a man asked in a very measured way.

"Yes."

"I'm…. Tanner. Is it… okay to come by… tomorrow at… nine?"

After confirming with Brianne that she could drive him to the farm in the morning, Brighton said, "Of course. I'll meet you here at the farm. Do you have the address?"

"Yes." He expected the man to repeat it to him, but he didn't.

"All right. I'll see you then." Brighton wondered what was up. Arthur had said his cousin didn't talk much. Suddenly he didn't have the greatest feeling about this.

Brighton sat for a few minutes until guilt over doing nothing while Brianne worked got the better of him. He leaned on his cane and opened the door. His grandfather thought he could do this or he wouldn't have left him the farm, and Brianne thought he could as well, so he needed to gird himself and just do it.

Brighton walked to the base of the stairs and looked upward. He took the first step. "Bree," he called. She appeared at the top of the stairs. "Come take my cane." She hurried down the stairs and took the cane from his hand. Then he put both hands on the banister and made his way up the steps.

"Why are you doing this?" Brianne asked when he was halfway up.

"Because I need to get around my own damn house if I'm going to live here." He didn't mean to snap, but it came out that way. Brighton was sweating by the time he made it to the top. He took his cane when Brianne offered it. "So, what are we doing?"

They spent some time cleaning a few of the rooms of dust and cobwebs. He mostly stripped beds and cleaned out drawers of linens that had seen better days. Brianne good-naturedly went up and down the stairs for him. "I think I need something to eat, and we've done enough," Brighton declared, stifling a cough. The dust was becoming too much for both of them. They had found some fans and had placed them in various windows to blow the air out of the house, and that helped.

"At least I got a room cleaned that you can use if you like." She gathered the supplies and placed them in the bathroom. "I'm filthy and need a shower." Brianne took Brighton's cane and his arm and helped him down the stairs, which was much easier than going up. "I just have one question: After I shower and change, where are you taking me for dinner?"

They reached the first floor without incident. "Wherever you'd like." Brighton took his cane and started for the front door. "But before I feed you, we need to make sure the animals are fed and inside before we leave for the night."

"Slave driver," Brianne quipped and hurried out to the barn. He heard her inside, calling and swearing, but she eventually returned. "They're in. None of them wanted to come until they heard the food. Everything is closed up, but I'm afraid the pens will need to be cleaned soon. And I draw the line at poop shoveling."

Brighton rolled his eyes. "I used to change you when you were a baby."

"Don't go there," Brianne warned. "You used that for years, but it isn't going to work anymore and neither is the story about the time I wet you. Guilt all you want—I'm not cleaning pens. Did you lock the house?"

"I will." He turned and closed the door then used the key the lawyer had given him to lock the door. "I think I should have the locks changed. I probably should have had that done today." He chewed on his lower lip. "I'll see to it tomorrow."

"If anything's missing we'll call the police and tell them what happened. They'll search Vera and Raymond's house so fast. They'd be stupid to try again." She paused, shaking her head. "Do you want to stay?"

"No. I want to go home." It had been a hell of a day, and Brighton needed a chance to think. "Come on. You can clean up at my place, and I'll order delivery. We can relax, and you can tell me about what you're interested in studying." Most of the time he had no idea what the hell she was talking about when it came to her work, but he always listened.

"Nope. I want to watch mindless television and think about nothing."

"Amen." That was the best idea he'd heard all day.

BRIANNE ENDED up spending the night on his sofa. They stayed up late and were falling asleep already, so he wasn't about to let her drive home that late. In the morning, after working the kinks out of his leg, Brighton dressed and made breakfast. It wasn't much, just bacon and eggs, but the scent had Brianne sniffing around the kitchen before her eyes were fully open. "God...."

"Sit, eat. Then we'll go."

"What time is it?" Brianne looked around for the clock.

"Eight. Tanner is coming to the farm at nine." Brighton put eggs on each plate along with some bacon. Then he added extra slices to Brianne's plate and handed it to her. Brighton knew the way to her heart: pork. She ate, still half-asleep, leaning over the table.

"I can't believe you got me up at the ass crack of dawn." Brianne wasn't a morning person.

"Please. It's eight, and I fed you." Brighton chewed on a slice of bacon.

"You're forgiven."

"Good, because we need to go in ten minutes." Brighton backed out of the line of fire and finished eating. Then he carried his dishes to the sink and waited for Brianne to finish. He put her dishes in the sink as well, and she humphed away, returning a few minutes later dressed but looking like hell.

"You're on your own today. I have things I have to do, but I'll come back to the farm before dinner and bring you home. I suggest you make sure you have something to eat."

"I'll order delivery," he quipped. They left his apartment, and she drove him to the farm. Brighton thanked her and got an unintelligible response from her. "At least help with the animals before you leave."

She turned off the engine and unfastened her seat belt, muttering the entire time. She didn't stop as she went to the barn or let up as she was opening doors and shooing the "beasts" outside. "They have water and feed. The rest is up to you. I'll see you later."

Brighton met her at the barn door and saw her stop, eyes widening. "What is it?" he asked as he followed her stare. "Oh...," Brighton added as one of the biggest men he'd ever seen walked down the drive in a cowboy hat, tight jeans hugging tree-trunk thighs, and a flannel shirt that look about ready to bust at the seams if the man breathed too deep. "Jesus," he whispered, watching as the man got closer. Brianne, who had been in an all-fired hurry to get away, suddenly stood stock-still. Not that Brighton could blame her. He blinked twice and stepped out of the barn, taking slow steps as he leaned on his cane. The man got close enough for Brighton to see blond hair poking out from under his hat and eyes as blue as the summer sky.

"Hello," the man said in a deep resonant voice. "I'm T-Tanner."

Brighton leaned on his cane, breathing hard, his mouth dry. Damn, the man was gorgeous in a rugged, had-a-hard-life kind of way. He pushed those thoughts aside, though, because they weren't appropriate on so many levels. First thing, this guy could snap him like a twig if he wanted, and second, hell, if he hired this man, then he wasn't doing anything with an employee. *Stop*, he silently yelled at himself. He was getting way ahead of things.

"I'm Brighton, and it appears I've inherited this place, but as you can probably guess, farm chores aren't something I can really do." Brighton began moving toward the house. "How did you get here?"

Tanner pointed toward a motorcycle parked out near the road. Brighton wondered why he'd parked it way out there but didn't ask. And Tanner didn't seem too keen on talking.

"I'm Brianne, his sister." Brianne reached to shake Tanner's hand. Tanner looked uncomfortable but shook her hand.

"Didn't you have things to do?" Brighton asked Brianne. She smacked him on the shoulder.

"I'll see you later," Brianne said, laughing as she walked to her car. Brighton waved as she got in and then drove away. Then he turned back to Tanner. "Can we go talk on the porch? I need to sit down. My leg hurts because I've been standing too long." He hobbled across the yard and climbed the two steps, then sat down in the rocking chair. There were days when he felt so damned old. Brighton motioned to the other chair, and Tanner perched on the edge of it like he was ready to run away at any second. "Arthur told me that you worked on a ranch in Montana."

Tanner nodded and reached up to lift his hat off his head. He placed it in his lap and nodded again. Brighton got no further answer.

"What kind of work did you do?"

"Ranch... stuff."

Brighton waited but didn't get any further elaboration. "Did you make repairs?"

Tanner nodded.

"Take care of horses and animals?"

Tanner nodded again without speaking, but his attention was clearly on Brighton.

"I need someone to feed and clean up in the barn and help with repairs around here. My grandfather hadn't been able to do a lot of things, and it's hard for me to haul and carry." It was hard for him to know he was getting his point across. Arthur had said his cousin didn't talk much, but he hadn't said he was nearly mute. "Do you understand?"

Tanner opened his mouth, but no sound came out at first. "Yes. I can... help." Tanner stood up, and without any further word, he walked over toward the barn and disappeared inside. Brighton sat a minute and was about to get up to see what was happening when he saw Tanner hauling a wheelbarrow full of mucked bedding out of the barn. He looked around and must have seen the muck pile. Tanner emptied it and returned to the barn without a word.

Brighton wasn't quite sure what had happened, but it seemed he'd hired himself some help. He'd have to explain to Tanner what he needed, but from the looks of things Tanner knew what he was doing and was willing to get his hands dirty. Brighton could do some things on his own, but many were beyond his capabilities. One thing he needed to do was to get Internet and his work equipment set up in the house if he was going to be spending his days here. For the first time since speaking with the lawyer, he felt that things just might work out. But then again, things had a habit of going to hell just when he thought he was out of the woods.

CHAPTER 2

TANNER HOUGHTON continued working, breathing a silent sigh of relief that it looked like he was about to get a job. He'd been trying to find something for a month, and what little money he'd arrived with from Montana was very quickly drying up, and soon he wouldn't be able to eat. When the… mess had happened out West—No, he didn't even like to think about that. It hurt in so many fucking ways. He dug his shovel into the dirty bedding of the goat pen and hoisted the heavy, wet straw into the wheelbarrow, the strain of the work therapeutic and soothingly familiar. Tanner had worked his entire life. His mama had taught him to always work hard, and her words rang in his head as he scooped the last of the bedding. "Son, you'll…." His mother never quite knew how to tell him bad news sometimes. "You're never going to be able to work with people, so eat up, grow strong, and work hard." Then she'd placed a heaping plate of food in front of him. Tanner paused a second to think about her before picking up the wheelbarrow handles and making the trip back out of the barn and around to the small muck area.

He wanted to ask Brighton, the man he'd talked to earlier, if there was a place he should spread this rather than just piling it up, but he'd have to think on that. Tanner didn't want to try talking to him much. Brighton might not keep him on if he found out Tanner was what most people he knew called a dummy. He made a trip back into the barn and found some bales of straw. He was finishing the last pen, but he would use the last of the straw, so he needed to let Brighton know.

Once he was done, Tanner took a look around the smallish barn and smiled as he inhaled. Nothing, in his opinion, rivaled the smell of a clean barn, except maybe the smell of open land just after a spring rain when everything was clean and just set to burst open.

"Do you want some lunch?"

Tanner started slightly and nodded his answer. He'd been so deep in his own thoughts that he hadn't heard Brighton come up behind him. Tanner turned and stopped himself from smiling at the slight man with Big Sky blue eyes and hair the color of his favorite chestnut horse back at the ranch in Montana. Lucy had been the sweetest thing. To him, anyway. She hated everyone else, nipped and fought them tooth and nail, but not Tanner. He'd understood her and treated her special. Since leaving, he'd wondered more than once if she was okay.

"I only have the stuff for sandwiches here. My sister was good enough to make sure I wouldn't starve. I hope that's okay. Come up to the house in a few minutes." Brighton's lips curled downward as he took a step. Tanner wasn't sure if Brighton was in pain or if it was the thought of having lunch with him that made him look that way. Tanner pushed that notion away. Brighton had just met him, and Tanner needed to remember that not everyone was like the other hands at the ranch, who would rather die than sit next to him in case they caught whatever it was they thought was wrong with Tanner.

"…Thank you." He always had to think carefully before starting sentences like that. Brighton turned and slowly walked back to the house. It was almost painful for Tanner to watch. Tanner had no doubt that Brighton was in pain. The muscles in his back, neck, and legs appeared to scream with tension, the way you could feel a horse go lame throughout its entire body. Tanner wanted to help somehow, but he was pretty sure that would be intruding. He watched Brighton until he'd almost reached the house and then turned and went back into the barn.

When he was done, Tanner put away all the tools where he'd found them along with the wheelbarrow and then walked across the yard to the house.

He stood on the front porch, unsure if he should knock on the screen door, just go in, or wait for Brighton. He decided to knock and heard labored footsteps and the tap… tap… of the cane on the floor. "I should have left the door unlocked," Brighton said and unlatched the door before pushing it open. "I'm so used to living in the city that I lock all the doors behind me."

Tanner nodded. It had been a month since he'd lived anywhere that wasn't open space, and he missed it something awful. This wasn't exactly the kind of wide-open space he was used to, where he could stand in one spot and turn in every direction and see nothing but the land stretching from horizon to horizon. That wasn't happening here, but at least there were trees and green between them and the ugly blue condo things. They looked like the dollhouse his sister had had when she was a kid—garish and fake. He stepped inside the house and followed Brighton through to the kitchen and sat at the old Formica table at one end. A plate of sandwiches sat on the counter. Brighton went to get them, but Tanner jumped up and hurried over, picked up the plate and the glasses that sat next to it, and brought them to the table.

"There's iced tea in the fridge." Brighton pulled out one of the chairs and sat down. "Sometimes I feel like an old man." Tanner pulled open the door and pulled out an old green glass pitcher just like the one his mama had once had. Tanner turned and nodded his understanding, closing the door. "I have good days and bad days. Today is one of the bad ones," Brighton said. He leaned his cane against the wall and grew quiet.

Tanner poured the tea and took his seat, waiting for Brighton to start. His stomach called out for food, but he did as his mama had always told him and waited for everyone else. Brighton took half of what appeared to be a ham sandwich, and Tanner took one as well. As soon as he took a bite, the mayo and spicy mustard filled his mouth, and he hummed. With the ice broken, Tanner tucked in to the food. He was a big guy with an appetite to match, but he restrained himself so he wouldn't look like a pig.

Brighton ate one sandwich and then sat back and drank his tea. "Eat all you like," Brighton encouraged, and Tanner went to work on the remaining food. "They're nothing fancy."

"I ain't been eating s… s… so good lately." He blushed a little and grew quiet again.

"Arthur said you were quiet. Is it because of your stutter?" Brighton asked.

Tanner nodded. People had made fun of him when he was a kid, and his teachers had seemed to think it was their challenge to "cure" him. They'd all had their ideas, but most of them only made him self-conscious, and so he stuttered more. "Yeah."

"I used to stutter when I was young. My mom sent me to a speech therapist, and she helped me. I still trip over words sometimes." Brighton smiled. "So you have no need to feel bad or think I'll judge you because of it. It took a long time before I was comfortable talking to most people."

"Lots of… p… people tried to help. N… none d… d… did." Tanner breathed gently once he'd gotten out the thought.

"Are you interested in the job?" Brighton asked, and Tanner nodded. "We'll need to work out your hours. I'll need someone each day to care for the animals." He assumed Tanner had a place to live.

"O… k-kay," Tanner agreed.

"So did you find everything you needed in the barn?" Brighton asked. Tanner nodded. "Was there anything we need?"

"Straw and h-hay."

"All right. Go ahead and make a list. I'll have to see if I can figure out where I can get them." Brighton sighed. "I can't drive, so…. There is a truck." Tanner pointed to himself, his mouth full. "I was hoping you'd do the driving, at least for now. I think we may also need some feed for the animals. I've been looking through my grandfather's papers to see if I could figure out where he bought supplies. I found a receipt for feed, so I think I'll call them and see if they can help with the other things too."

That sounded logical to Tanner. "What else?" Tanner asked. He thought about getting a piece of paper to write down what he wanted to say.

"I'm not sure what you're asking," Brighton said.

"Chores." He'd had to think of a word that was easy for him to say. "Repairs."

Brighton nodded. "There are lots of them. Let's start with the pens. I want to make sure the animals are cared for and safe. Then I was hoping some repairs on the house could be done. I've been told there's also an orchard on part of the property, and the trees will probably need attention."

Tanner shook his head. "Trees." He'd never had any experience around trees. He could fix a lot of things and repair fences and stuff like that. He could do all kinds of other work too, but he didn't know anything about trees other than how to cut them down, and somehow he didn't think that was what Brighton had in mind.

"We'll figure it out. I have a computer, and I can look up on the Internet what to do. It can't be that hard."

Tanner wasn't so sure of that, but he nodded and finished drinking his tea. When he was done, Tanner took the dishes to the sink and then left the house. He went back over toward the barn and checked all the pens. Some of the fence posts were weak and would need to be replaced. He found a pencil and paper in the barn and made drawings of each pen, noting what he found. When he was done, he took the papers to the porch. Brighton sat in the old rocking chair, head back, eyes closed. Brighton sure was pretty when he was asleep. The tension around his eyes and mouth was gone. Maybe some of the pain that Brighton seemed to be in was eased when he was asleep. Tanner didn't want to disturb him, so he left quietly and returned to the barn. The building itself was in good shape, but one of the doors needed work, so Tanner hunted up tools and began making repairs.

The sun was bright, throwing off plenty of heat. Tanner heated up as he worked and eventually unbuttoned his shirt and threw it over one of the fence rails. He felt cooler, and it was nice to have the sun on his skin again. He'd often worked shirtless at the ranch. Other men had done the same—that is, until the mess started. Then Tanner had felt eyes on him all the time, and more often than not he'd tried to find chores that kept him away from the other hands.

That had only put him in harm's way more often. The whole situation had quickly become… well, a mess, and Tanner had felt he had to leave. Problem was, word spread, and he'd traveled farther and farther to find work until he'd finally talked to his cousin and had been convinced to try moving to the city.

He continued working and got the repair completed, along with a few others. After he finished the last one, Tanner stood, stretching his back to get the kink out. He turned and saw Brighton walking slowly across the yard. He wondered if he should put his shirt on but figured they were both guys, and there was nothing wrong with going shirtless when he was working. It was hot as all get out, and he'd been busy sweating up a storm. Tanner reached into his back pocket and pulled out his drawings. When Brighten got closer, he handed them to him so he could see what he needed.

"All right," Brighton said, appearing a little surprised. "They seem pretty decent, then, with just a few posts and rails to replace. Is the wire in good shape?" The pens were lined with a wire mesh on the inside so the smaller animals and babies couldn't get out.

Tanner made a waving motion with his hand, and Brighton nodded.

"I figured out where we can get what we need. It's about fifteen miles west. Grandpa had an account with them. If we take the truck, we can probably load it up and get the supplies brought back by the end of the day."

"Okay," Tanner agreed. He walked over to where he'd left his shirt. Then he checked that all the animals had food and water before following Brighton to the garage. Inside was a newish truck. Brighton handed him the keys and then climbed in the passenger side.

As Tanner got in, Brighton's phone rang. Tanner closed the door and started the engine while Brighton answered the phone. "I'm fine, Brianne. ... Tanner and I are going to get supplies. Have you called the attorney?" Tanner pulled out of the garage and turned around in the yard before heading down the drive. He wasn't sure where to go, but Brighton motioned with his hand to turn right. "Well, she doesn't get to make those decisions all by herself. ... I'll call Aunt Vera and get this settled. I want you to attend your graduation and so would Grandpa. You heard what he said. He was proud of you for going to school and making something of yourself." There was a hitch in Brighton's voice. "I like to think that Grandpa will be there right alongside you."

Brighton hung up and turned to him. "Go partway around the traffic circle up ahead and then get on the highway. Take it to 70 and go in the direction of Frederick. After about five miles or so we'll need to get off again, and the hardware and supply store should be nearby, according to their directions."

Tanner nodded and drove. He didn't know his way around the city very well. More times than not, he got lost as hell. But it was great spending time on his bike, though he liked it more in Montana, where he could go as fast as he wanted when he needed speed.

Brighton made another call as they approached the freeway. "Aunt Vera, it's Brighton." He was quiet. "Mr. Granger told me you've moved the service to Sunday."

Tanner merged into traffic. Whatever was going on sounded like family drama. He hated that stuff. Tanner's own family was full of infighting and this faction against that faction. But no matter what, he and his mother had always been out of favor with everyone, or nearly everyone. His cousins Arthur and Riva had always been good to him, though.

"Brianne is graduating on Sunday, and she's going." A brief pause. "No, she isn't going to give it up, and it has nothing to do with her being more important than Grandpa. It has to do with you being a petty old bat. Grandpa would want her to go, and so do I. Now, the funeral will be on Saturday afternoon, with visitation before. If I have to call Arthur...." Another pause, and Tanner changed lanes to get into position to make the shift to the other highway. "I know you're angry about the farm and all, but that's the way it is. Grandpa set it up this way, so if you want to be angry with someone, be mad at him, but don't take it out on the rest of us." Brighton stopped once again. "All right. Here's the deal. You want to play this way, I'll call you on it. The funeral will be Saturday, and you will make all the arrangements like you promised. In return, I won't call the police and have you arrested for attempted robbery."

Tanner glanced over at Brighton—the fire in his eyes was exciting. He'd been pretty when he was asleep. But damn, the set of his jaw and the heat burning in Brighton's eyes sent a jolt of attraction through him. Tanner turned away and concentrated on the road. He needed to get his head in the right place. It was this sort of thinking that had gotten him in trouble before, and he wasn't going to let it happen again. He needed this job.

"Don't try me. ... I know we're family, but you crossed a line, and you're trying to do it again." Brighton sighed. "Just make the arrangements... and no games. No one needs that." Brighton listened. "This isn't about you or me or Brianne. This is about everyone in the family being able to say good-bye to Grandpa." His tone was much lighter now.

Tanner concentrated on the highway, and after a few minutes, Brighton hung up and put his head back against the seat and said, "Sometimes family sucks." Tanner knew that sentiment well, but he kept quiet and drove, refusing to go down memory lane. After all, his was full of potholes. Tanner exited the highway when Brighton told him to and followed his directions.

He pulled into an old farm-supply store that looked like it had been there since the Depression and hadn't been painted in twenty years, at least. Tanner parked near the door and then got out. He hurried around the truck and pulled open Brighton's door. He waited for Brighton to get out and followed him to the door, where he held it for him.

"Can I help you?" a man who looked nearly as old as the store asked when they stepped inside.

"I'm Brighton McKenzie. I called earlier."

"And you're the young man who's taking over for your grandpa? I'm Earl, and I think I used to remember when he brought you in. You were knee-high then. You used to stare up at the gumball machine but never asked to have one."

"But you always gave me one anyway," Brighton said with a grin. After a second Brighton turned to his new hand. "This is Tanner. He's helping me at the farm." Brighton leaned a little more heavily on his cane. "There aren't many physical things I can do." He motioned downward. "Anyway, we have a list of things we need and Grandpa's truck to haul them back in."

"Then let's get you squared away. You said on the phone you needed hay and straw. I can set you up with a load and deliver it on Monday, so take with you what you think you'll need till then. As for the rest, hand me the list. I'm sure we can help with that."

Brighton gave him the list. "Thanks, Earl. I'm a little lost when it comes to all this." Brighton seemed a little smaller and looked much more tired than he had just an hour earlier.

"You know you could sell and make a lot of money. You've got prime land in a great location," Earl said.

"Yeah, but then it would be gone, and it was important to Grandpa. Otherwise he could have sold the land and made the money himself. Then he could have lived an easier life anywhere he wanted." Brighton sighed and looked squarely at the older man. "He kept the land and left it to me for a reason. So I'm going to try to figure out what that was."

Tanner found himself smiling. He liked that Brighton cared for his grandfather enough to do what he wanted… or at least try, even if it was hard for him with his leg.

"My grandson is going to take over for me here." Earl turned away. "Johnny," he called, and a kid about college age came out of the back. "Can you help load the truck? Here's the list of what they need for today." Earl handed it to the man.

"Drive 'round back, and I'll get you loaded up," Johnny told him, and Tanner left and drove the truck around the building. He found Johnny by a pile of posts and pulled to a stop. The two of them loaded what was needed. Johnny rambled on about what he was going to do with the place and the ideas he had. Tanner listened and said nothing. He was used to people talking at him. They did it all the time. He'd quickly found out that if he didn't say anything, a lot of people would just keep talking and not even notice. "You don't talk much, do you?" Johnny finally asked once they were nearly done with the posts.

Tanner shook his head as he lifted first a bale of straw and one of hay into the truck bed.

"Can you talk?" Johnny asked.

"Yes."

"One of those strong silent types." Johnny smiled. "Never could do that. I talk all the time. Grandpa says I talk way too much. Says I hate the quiet and have to fill the space. Maybe he's right."

"Maybe," Tanner agreed and said no more. Those were easy words for him and didn't make him sound dumb.

"Well, that should about do it," Johnny said with a smile. "Let's head around the front. We can settle up, and you two can be on your way."

Tanner got in the truck and started the engine right away, cranking the AC to try to cool himself. He lifted his arms and let the cool air wash over his skin before driving around to the front of the store. Brighton opened the door almost as soon as the truck stopped.

Tanner wondered if something was wrong, but he sat quietly while Brighton pulled himself inside.

"We'll deliver the rest of what you need," Earl said once Brighton was inside and had rolled down the window. "Get off that leg. In the future you can call in what you need, and Johnny will deliver, if you want. It's no problem."

"Thanks, Earl." Brighton rubbed his bad leg. "I'm really okay. It's not your fault at all, and I didn't get hurt, just a little scared." Brighton smiled and shook Earl's hand. The old man stepped away from the truck, and Brighton rolled up the window. Tanner pulled out and made a left turn to head back to the highway.

That lame-horse look was back. Brighton's entire body radiated pain. Eventually he pulled out his phone and pressed a couple of buttons. "Brianne. We're on our way back to the farm now. Yeah, I fell at the supply store. ... No, it wasn't their fault. ... My leg aches, and I probably bruised something. No. I think I'm going to sleep at the farm. Would you bring my laptop from the apartment? The cable people are going to come and hook stuff up this afternoon, so I can work there, and that way you won't have to drive me back and forth."

Tanner thought he heard laughter from the phone but wasn't sure. He remembered the pretty girl from when he arrived. She'd seemed nice, and he'd seen the way she'd looked at him. It made him want to run for the hills. It was apparent she liked him, or at least the way he looked. But Tanner had learned long ago that girls were trouble—at least they were for him.

"I'll be fine. You cleaned up a room for me, and I'll make it up the stairs on my own. It's time. ... Okay. I'll see you in a little while." Brighton hung up and once again rested his head back against the seat. Tanner remembered how to get back to the farm, so he simply drove, and since Brighton's eyes were closed, he kept glancing at him.

This wasn't good. He wished he knew what it was about Brighton that had captured his interest so he could push it away. These kinds of feelings always seemed to bring trouble for him. Tanner forced his attention back to the highway. Cars zoomed past, but he didn't speed up. He was going the speed limit, and with a load like he was carrying that was fast enough. He made the switch to the other highway and then got off near the same place where he'd gotten on and made the turn toward the farm. As he turned into the farm drive, Brighton opened his eyes and groaned. "Who's that?" A car was parked near the house. "By the way, you don't need to park your bike there. It might get hit or something. Park it in the garage."

"The noise?" At the ranch he'd never been allowed to bring the bike close to the house. The missus hadn't liked the noise. Tanner hadn't even realized how engrained it was.

"Don't worry about it." Brighton yawned, and Tanner pulled next to the other car as the door opened and a man got out. Brighton groaned again, and Tanner wondered what was going on. "Let me out, and then you can take the supplies over to the barn."

Tanner nodded and waited for Brighton. He was curious about what was happening, but he moved the truck the short distance to the barn and then got out and started unloading.

A raised voice reached his ears. "Mom and Dad were good to you!" Tanner paused from where he'd been pulling posts out of the back of the truck. "You always were a little shit who thought he was better than everyone else." The man stepped closer to Brighton. Tanner paused with his hand on a post.

"And you were a bully." Brighton's voice reached him as well. Tanner had to give Brighton credit—he didn't back away. The two men glared at each other.

"This place is too much for you." The man waved his arms around. "You can't even walk. How are you going to make a go of this?" He was practically shouting now. Tanner pulled off his gloves and threw them into the bed of the truck. Then he marched over to where Brighton stood. Neither of them saw him at first. But then the stranger glanced his way and stopped mid-yell, mouth hanging open.

"This is Tanner," Brighton said. "He's helping me out here. Tanner, this is my cousin, Mick. He came to give me his opinion on what I should do."

Mick didn't say anything for a while and then turned back to Brighton. "This place isn't big enough to be financially viable. Grandpa had talked of selling a few years ago. That's what you should do."

"Why does everyone care what I do? Grandpa left me the farm, and I'm going to stay here and see what I can do. It's what he wanted me to do. I know your mom and dad are disappointed that they aren't going to get the money they would by selling, but Grandpa left them something, just like he remembered you. So maybe you should all be happy with what you got." Brighton sighed again. "I'm going inside. I'm tired, and this conversation isn't going to get us anywhere." Brighton turned, and Tanner saw Mick clench his fists.

"You sanctimonious little shit. We should be happy? We got the scraps, and you got everything, and we all should be happy with that?" Mick hurried over to where Brighton was starting up the steps. Without thinking Tanner lunged, grabbing Mick by the arm. Mick tried to pull away, but Tanner held tight.

"That's enough, Mick. We aren't kids any longer, and you can't get your way by hitting or thumping the rest of us. You need to grow up." Brighton's eyes blazed from where he stood on the edge of the porch. "You can let him go," he said to Tanner. "He won't try anything. Like most bullies, Mick's basically a coward at heart. If he thinks someone will stand up to him, he folds like a house of cards. You don't scare me any longer. When we were kids, I used to want to be your friend. I needed you then." Brighton lifted his cane off the decking. "I'd just lost my parents, and you and the rest of the shits you call siblings made Brianne's life and my life as close to hell as you could. So think about that before you come around here telling anyone what we should and shouldn't do." Brighton stepped back and lowered himself in the chair. "Now go. And tell the rest of them to leave me alone."

A car pulled in. It was the one Tanner had seen earlier in the day. The car braked to a halt, and the lady he'd met earlier, Brighton's sister, hurried up to them. Tanner let go of Mick's arm and stepped away.

"What are you doing here?" Brianne asked. She was a spitfire—she got right up in Mick's scowly face.

"I tried to talk some sense into your brother."

"Since when did you have any?" Brianne countered, and Tanner covered his mouth to keep from laughing. "What happens with the farm is Brighton's decision, and all you lot are going to respect it and leave him alone." She stepped forward. "Unless you're keen to pick up a shovel and pitch in."

Mick backed away in a huff and walked to his car, then drove away. Tanner watched him go along before turning to head to the barn.

"Thank you for helping him," Brianne said, and it took Tanner a few seconds to realize she was talking to him. He stopped and nodded before going back to work. "I knew that would make him leave. If there's work, he's gone."

Their voices faded, and Tanner got back to work unloading the truck. He wasn't sure how late he was expected to work. At the ranch it was often sunup to sundown. There was too much to do and never enough hours in the day. Here there were things to do, but it wasn't like there were that many demands.

Tanner unloaded the posts, hauled the hay and straw into the barn, and then made sure all the tools were put away. Everything had to be in its place; otherwise it would bother him. When he was done and everything was settled to his satisfaction, he made sure all the critters had food and water and then closed up the barn.

Brighton sat on the porch alone, a computer resting on his lap. He appeared content. A truck with the name of a cable company blazoned on the side was parked in the drive. "Would you like some tea?" Brighton asked. "Brianne made some. You have to be thirsty." Brighton stood and went inside.

Tanner stood on the porch for a few minutes, then finally sat in one of the other rocking chairs. Brighton returned and handed him a glass. "Thank you." Tanner drank most of the tea in two gulps. He hadn't realized how thirsty he was until the liquid hit his throat. "Good."

"Did you get everything done?"

Tanner nodded.

"Where did you put the posts?"

Tanner tried to think how he could convey his thoughts without talking. "Around the... the c... c... c... corner."

"Good." Brighton smiled, and Tanner scowled as he realized Brighton had done that on purpose, to get him to talk. "You have a nice voice. I like hearing it." Tanner rolled his eyes. "You do."

Tanner nodded and finished the last of his tea. "I will go n... now."

"I'll see you tomorrow," Brighton said lightly. Tanner was about to ask if he should take his glass inside, but Brighton held out his hand, so Tanner handed it to him and then got up to leave. He walked down the drive to where he'd parked his bike near one of the trees. As he carefully put his hat in his saddlebag, he looked up toward the house and saw Brighton watching him. Tanner wasn't quite sure what that meant. Brighton continued to look at him, and even at this distance, Tanner could feel the heat from Brighton's eyes. It sent an answering surge of heat through him, and Tanner had to look away. He did not want to be riding home with a woody. Things could get painful.

Tanner started the engine and eased the bike onto the drive and then out into traffic. The wind rushing through his clothes and his hair felt great. He knew he should wear a helmet and safety gear, but it was so hot, and he needed the feel of air and openness. This whole place, except for the farm, felt closed in and stifling to him. As he rode farther, the homes and lots got larger. Eventually he turned into a drive and parked next to the Lexus that Arthur's wife, Alicia, drove. Arthur had agreed to let him rent the room above his garage.

When the house had been built, Arthur had said that he'd intended to use the room over the garage as a home office but never got around to setting it up. It had a bathroom, so Tanner had moved in and added a microwave and minifridge so his basic needs were covered. If he was there, he ate with Arthur, Alicia, and the boys. Tonight he was starved and tired as hell. He was used to working, and it wasn't like he'd put in a hard day. All he could figure was that he was getting soft.

"Uncle Tanner," Marky called as he raced out of the house in his sock feet. "Can I go for a ride?" He was five and a bundle of energy. With his dark hair and eyes, he was the spitting image of his Cuban mother.

"Don't bother your uncle right now," Alicia said from the door. "I'm sure he's tired, and you need to let him eat."

"Later," Tanner whispered, pleased he was able to get the word out without faltering. Sometimes it was easier around people he knew. They didn't make him feel as nervous or self-conscious about the way he spoke. He opened his saddlebag and pulled out his hat.

Marky hurried back to the house. His younger brother, Josh, stood next to his mother, holding her hand. He was shy and always stood back a little. Tanner went to him, lifted him into his arms, and whirled him around. Josh smiled and eventually laughed as Tanner tried to make him happy. Then Tanner placed him back on his feet, and both boys ran off inside the house.

"Arthur is still working, but I have dinner ready. The boys already ate." She led the way into the house and closed the door after him. Tanner wasn't sure Alicia liked him much. It was sometimes hard for him to tell. She didn't mind him playing with the boys, but she tended to stay away from him most of the time. He figured Arthur had told her what had happened and why he was here. Tanner couldn't expect him to keep it from her, he supposed.

"T... thank you." Unlike the boys, she made him nervous. There was no particular reason for it, but she did. Tanner took the seat she indicated, lifting his hat off his head. He set it aside, and Alicia brought him a plate. They didn't talk while he ate. She kept busy and left a few times to check on the boys. Once he was done, Tanner thanked her and said good night to the boys before heading up to his room above the garage.

For a man who was quiet and said very little, Tanner had a hard time adjusting to his own company sometimes. Sure, it had been quiet at the ranch, but there were always other people around, and when he was working, he'd usually worked with someone else. He liked peace, but hours of sitting in this one room, watching the boob tube or just sleeping…. He was lonely, and he knew it. Hell, Tanner had thought that he'd found someone who didn't think he was dumb and might have liked him for him. And maybe Royce *had* liked him, but he'd made his choice, and that meant Tanner had to go.

Tanner went right into the bathroom and stripped off his sweaty work clothes. Then he started the water and stepped under it. Man, that felt good. The water ran gray for a bit as the dirt rolled off him, and then he began cleaning up. He had a job, and he liked the man he was working for. Brighton seemed nice enough. For the millionth time, he wondered what had happened to him. There was such life and energy in his eyes, and yet sometimes he seemed so defeated. Tanner knew how that felt… for sure. He soaped up and washed his lower half. He was tired, but parts of him were up and ready. For the last little while, he would think of Royce and his compact, lean body. His was the only body other than his own that he'd ever gotten to know in that way. So when he felt that need, he recalled those images.

He wrapped his fingers around his cock, stroking long and slow, just the way he liked it. Damn, that felt good. He thought about Royce, and things were off to a good start just like they always were. But then, like a scratch on a record, everything derailed. Royce had walked away. Why in hell was he thinking of someone who didn't want him? His hand stopped, and Tanner's cock softened like someone had just thrown a bucket of cold water on him. He sighed and rinsed off. Then he turned off the water and stepped out of the tub. He grabbed a towel and dried off before hanging the towel back up and then returning to his small room to get dressed.

A car pulled into the drive as Tanner pulled on a T-shirt. He parted the curtains slightly and peered out. His young cousins crowded around Arthur's car, jumping up and down as he got out.

He greeted both of them and then herded the boys toward the front door. None of them looked up toward his window, and he'd bet they didn't give him another thought as they went about their happy evening. He knew they had their lives to live just as he did. It wasn't realistic for them to entertain and take care of him; that wasn't what he wanted. Tanner was a man, and he knew he had to build his own life. That was what he'd gone out West to do in the first place. He'd simply made one hell of a mess of it. That was all. Tanner let the curtain fall back into place. He lay down on the bed and watched television until he dozed off.

THE NEXT day he was at the farm bright and early. He turned off the road and coasted to a stop. The house looked shut up, and he didn't want to disturb Brighton if he was sleeping. Something told him Brighton didn't do much of that, especially judging by the way he seemed to doze off all the time. He walked the bike the rest of the way and parked it inside the garage. Then he headed to the barn and let the critters out into their pens. Well, not the goats. They were none too pleased, but he wanted to make the repairs on their pen first.

He got out the posts and crosspieces and started dismantling the area of the pen he'd need to get at. It took some digging, but eventually he got the bad posts out and the new ones set in the ground. Then he fixed the crosspieces and put the mesh into place. When he let the goats out, they explored their area like it was brand-new and then settled in to rest and roam. He petted a few of them, and they seemed docile enough. None of them tried to bite him or anything.

The sound of a slight shuffle told him Brighton was coming up behind him. "My grandmother was the one who loved goats. She used to say they reminded her of Grandpa. I think Grandpa kept them because of her." Brighton leaned heavily on his cane, looking like he was going to fall over at any second. "It looks good."

Tanner smiled and nodded his thanks.

"You need to talk to me, please."

"Okay." Tanner said, lifting his hand to scratch his head and then letting it fall back into place. "I don't have much to s... say."

Brighton smiled. "I bet you have plenty to say. You've just gotten used to remaining quiet and letting everyone else do the talking." Brighton wavered slightly, and Tanner jumped to his feet to steady him. "It's all right. I've gotten used to the weakness in my leg." Tanner rushed into the barn and carried out a bale of straw. He set it on the ground and motioned for Brighton to sit down. If he was going to stay, then Tanner needed to work and not worry that Brighton was going to fall over at any time. "It's prickly."

Tanner nodded, and the thought of where it was prickly made him grin.

"Did you grow up around here? I know that Arthur is your cousin, so...."

Tanner shook his head. "W... West Virginia. I grew up outside Wheeling." He picked up some posts and began laying them out near the sheep pen. It was in even worse shape than the goat pen. It was a blessing the sheep didn't stress the fence—otherwise they would have been wandering around the property. "My mom was different." Tanner kept his voice level and thought about each word before he said it. "She wasn't... she didn't get along with the rest of the family. Arthur and his sister, Riva, were my friends when we came here to visit. But they never came to Wheeling."

"Why?"

"Mom did the best she could, but we never had much." Tanner turned away. "Mostly I ate because of food s... stamps. Then Mom got a job—a good job—and things got better. We moved farther out. She ended up working in one of the mines. She was tough as nails, and she was determined to make a better life for us." He began speaking faster, stumbling over words, but he had to get it out or he'd never say it. "She breathed in too much of the air, and her lungs gave out when I was eighteen." Tanner picked up one of the posts and put it where it was needed. "I told her I would take care of myself, and she said if I worked in the mines, she would haunt me forever. So I decided after the funeral to go out West." He leaned against one of the solid posts. He never talked about himself with anyone and he wasn't sure why he was with Brighton, other than the fact that he'd asked and seemed willing to listen. "I had dreams of making my fortune and my mark, and instead I ended up back here with nothing." Tanner opened the gate and began herding the sheep inside the barn. They grumbled but finally ambled inside. Tanner closed the door and went to work dismantling the fencing so he could make repairs.

"You didn't return with nothing," Brighton began. "I was about to ask what happened, but I can tell you don't want to talk about it." He stood up, balancing on his cane. "I need to go back to the house." Tanner was about to put the bale of straw back in the barn, but Brighton stopped him. "I'll be back in a bit. So you can leave it." Brighton slowly walked back toward the house. Tanner watched until he reached the porch and then returned to his work.

The sun beat down, and Tanner lifted his hat off his head and wiped his brow. He needed to let the heat dissipate, but it wasn't working. After setting his hat on top of one of the posts, he tugged off his sweaty shirt and draped it over one of the cross braces and then plopped his hat back on his head. He returned to work.

"I brought you something to drink," Brighton said. Tanner looked up from where he was working. Brighton had his cane in one hand and a small cooler in the other, and he was staring at him. Tanner reached for his shirt but then stopped. He wasn't a blushing virgin, and it wasn't like he minded the way Brighton was watching him.

"Thank you." That wasn't necessary. But it was dang nice. Tanner was sweating up a storm. Brighton sat back down on the bale and opened the cooler. He handed Tanner a bottle of juice and took one for himself. Tanner opened his, drank most of it, and then went back to work. He needed to keep moving. Even though the sun was still shining, the feel of the air was changing. In the West, out on the land, he'd developed a feel for what was going to happen. There weren't weather reports available every five minutes, so you relied on your nose and the feel of the air. Tanner moved faster, replacing the posts as clouds began to gather. At first the sun dimmed slightly, but then the sky darkened.

Tanner finished the repair and then herded the goats inside. It wasn't hard. They knew something was coming. "You should go inside," he said to Brighton, looking up at the sky as the clouds thickened. "I'll get everything buttoned down."

Brighton stood and picked up the cooler. He carried it toward the house while Tanner got into gear. He finished getting all the animals bedded down. As he closed the barn door, thunder sounded in the distance, and the wind picked up. Tanner grabbed his shirt and made sure everything was where it was supposed to be before striding to the porch. He figured he could wait out the storm and go back to work.

"It looks bad. I have food ready," Brighton said from the doorway and held the screen open.

Tanner took off his hat, pulled on his shirt, and went inside.

Brighton motioned toward where they'd had lunch the day before. "I think we'd better eat now in case we lose power." Thunder rumbled outside, followed by lightning and more thunder. Tanner peered out the kitchen window. Thick clouds rolled forward, tumbling over each other. Lightning continued flashing, and within seconds the sky opened up in a deluge. The rain came down so hard Tanner could barely see the barn at all.

"Sit down and eat. Grandpa always said he lost power in a stiff breeze, so who knows how much longer we'll have lights." Tanner took a seat, and Brighton carried over a plate of sandwiches. "Sorry. I'm not much of a cook. Mom never really taught me, so I pretty much exist on food like this." A clap of thunder made them both jump. "I should go to the grocery store soon." Another clap of thunder split the air, and Brighton plopped into a chair.

The air crackled—that one was so close. Tanner hated storms like this. He'd encountered enough of them in Montana and during a short job in Wyoming. They always got to him. He got back up and peered out the window once again, chewing slightly on his lower lip. The rain was still coming down in sheets. Lightning flashed while he watched, and Tanner jumped back from the window, a streak still shining in the back of his eyes. The crack that followed hurt his ears, and Tanner ended up on the floor, holding his head.

"Are you okay?" Brighton hurried over, and Tanner felt Brighton join him on the floor. He didn't think how Brighton got there, only that he had. "Can you see?"

"It's blinky," Tanner said. He kept his eyes closed, and the line across his vision slowly began to fade.

"Can you hear me all right?" Brighton placed a hand on his shoulder. "Just stay where you are."

"Was anything hit?" Tanner asked. "If it was the barn, we gotta help the animals." Tanner tried to get up but didn't trust opening his eyes. Brighton leaned against him.

"I think the barn is still standing. I can see it through the window." Brighton leaned more heavily, and as he tried to get back on his feet, he said, "Yeah, it looks okay from here. Whatever it hit, it wasn't the barn, and it doesn't appear to be the house either, thank goodness. Can you stand?"

Tanner nodded and tried opening his eyes. The dark room swayed for a few seconds, and then things came into focus. He could see. He wasn't surprised to find the power had gone out. Slowly Tanner got to his feet. Brighton leaned against the counter, and Tanner peered over his shoulder. He inhaled and caught the scent of Brighton's manly yet sweet scent. Tanner backed away slightly. It was situations like this that had gotten him in trouble in the past. "The barn is okay," Tanner said in agreement and pointed just behind it. "The tree." It had been split down the middle. Some of the limbs could have fallen on the barn, but the main body seemed to have fallen on open ground.

"Let's finish our lunch." Brighton turned around, and Tanner looked him right in the eyes. Neither of them moved, and Tanner stifled the gasp that threatened to well up from inside him. He wondered what Brighton would taste like. He moved a little closer as Brighton's lips parted. The storm continued raging outside, but it seemed to have faded away as far as Tanner was concerned, replaced by the beating of his own heart and the blood racing through his veins.

Brighton blinked but didn't look away. Tanner moved closer still. He wanted to touch and taste, but his arms remained at his side, and he only moved so close. Brighton had to come partway. He couldn't do it all and risk getting the signals wrong again. Neither of them moved. There was another flash of lightning, and a clap of thunder rattled the windows. Tanner didn't move, his lips parted slightly, breath held. Then he blinked a few times, remembering himself and what he was doing, and backed away. This was not a good idea.

"Why?" Brighton breathed just under his breath as he moved back slightly. "You don't want to do this with me." Brighton moved toward the table. He sat back down and stared at the half-eaten sandwich still on his plate. Brighton didn't look up at him or move for a long time. When he did, he picked up the sandwich, took a single bite, and then set it back on the plate. "That was nice of you, Tanner, but you don't want to kiss me."

He didn't understand. Maybe he never would. Nothing but trouble had followed him since Tanner had figured out that he liked boys instead of girls. He'd never told his mother, and he liked to think she would have understood and not judged him for it, but everyone else seemed to. At least Brighton hadn't called him unnatural and run him off the farm. "What's wrong with you?" Tanner whispered without thinking and then realized the words had come out as smooth as silk, without the hint of a stutter or hesitation. "I mean, what d... do you... think is wrong?"

Brighton looked up from his plate. "You've seen me, Tanner. I can barely walk, and even standing up for more than a few minutes is nearly impossible. It's been this way for over a year since the accident, even with additional surgery a few months ago, and it hasn't gotten better. Oh, the pain has lessened some, but my leg hasn't gotten stronger like everyone said it would." Brighton looked miserable, slumped forward, his lips turned downward, gaze turned toward the floor. "I used to hope I could walk again like everyone else. But I don't think that's going to happen."

Tanner had no words of comfort. He knew how Brighton felt. He remembered lying in his bed in his tiny room while his mother sat up in the other one, doing all kinds of things to try to make money. She sold jewelry, knitted, sewed doll clothes—whatever she could. He used to lie there and pray to Baby Jesus to help him talk right. He was eight years old, and his speech had gotten worse and worse. His teachers tried to help, but the more everyone tried—that he tried—the harder things got. He prayed to be like everyone else night after night, but nothing changed. Things never changed for him.

"Sorry," Tanner said just above a whisper. His throat ached, but not in the usual way. A lump formed, and he swallowed around it. "I h… h… had a teacher who said I c… c… could do anything I wanted if I p… put my mind to it. He used to hit my desk when I stuttered. He'd tell me that I wasn't trying hard enough when I caught my words." Tanner paused. "He was full of shit!"

"Yes, he was," Brighton agreed.

"So are you if you t… t… think your leg will j… just get better." Tanner didn't want to make Brighton mad. "They have therapy."

"I went, but it didn't do anything. My leg ached all the time, and it didn't get better. All it did was hurt." Brighton shifted in his chair. The storm seemed to be passing over. The lightning still flashed, but the thunder didn't come as quickly behind it. Tanner didn't move from where he stood near the sink. He was sort of afraid to.

"My head used to hurt after one of my teachers thought hitting me would help."

Brighton's head snapped upward. "They hit you?"

Tanner nodded. "That was easier sometimes than being told I was d... dumb." He hated that word so much. It had been thrown in his direction by so many people in his life that truthfully, he'd begun to believe they were right. He was a dummy who couldn't talk right.

"They were wrong. All of them were wrong. And you aren't dumb. Stuttering is a speech impediment, nothing more. It isn't a measure of intelligence or heart. It doesn't mean you can't do anything you want or be as smart and funny as anyone else."

"Your leg means the same thing," Tanner countered. "It doesn't have to stop you from being you."

The kitchen windows began to lighten as the worst of the storm passed. The rain continued, and Tanner wondered what he should do. He could go to the barn, but there weren't many chores he needed to do there. Everything left to do was outside. "I could do some things in here if you like," he offered. He needed something to do, because the way Brighton was looking at him made him shift from foot to foot.

"Sit down if you like. It's still raining, and we don't have any power. The tools and stuff are in the basement, and you'll break your neck trying to find them down there in the dark. This should be over soon."

"Okay," Tanner agreed. "Tea?" he asked, pointing to the refrigerator.

"Thanks."

Tanner got up and retrieved the pitcher from the fridge, keeping the door open no longer than he had to. He poured them both glasses and sat back down. He drank and alternated between looking out the window and glancing at Brighton. He found he was now fascinated with Brighton's lips and the little divot in the center of his upper lip. He once again wondered what he would taste like and how it would be to kiss him. Of course, Brighton was his boss, and he needed the job.

Brighton's words rang in his ear: *You don't want to kiss me.* Brighton hadn't said that he didn't want to kiss Tanner. Not that it mattered. No matter what Brighton actually said, Tanner figured it was Brighton's way of telling him he wasn't interested in a dummy.

THE RAIN continued for quite a while. Tanner couldn't just sit around, and once it slowed enough, he left and hurried out to the barn. It truly was okay, and the critters, while nerved up, were fine. He gave them a little extra feed, and that calmed them down. A little. Since working outside wasn't possible, he began organizing things in the barn. One section was a jumble of things. It looked like the barn version of the junk closet. Tanner began pulling things out. There were broken chairs, an old bicycle that had seen better days but looked intact, and some buckets with cracks and holes. What was obviously trash he set aside to be hauled away, but the other things he organized and put to the side, figuring Brighton might want to see them.

Other than the shuffling of the animals in their pens, it was quiet. It wasn't until he began to get warm that he realized the sun had come out. The barn air became close and sticky fast. He didn't want to let the animals outside. The pens were a muddy mess, so he opened the windows and door to let the air circulate.

By the time he was done, Tanner was covered in sweat even though he hadn't worked that hard. The humidity was stifling. At one point Tanner wondered if Brighton was still in the house. He peered out from the barn door. As he watched, Brighton came out and sat on the porch with his computer on his lap. Tanner peered at him for a few minutes. He still wondered what fascinated him so much about Brighton. He wished like hell he could just do his work and not wonder about him all the time.

He never learned. He'd been just as interested in Royce, except Royce had been aloof and distant at first. It had taken time for Royce to pay attention to him. Brighton was nice and listened to what Tanner had to say. Very few people seemed to care or took the time to listen to him. Brighton was willing. He listened.

But nothing was going to happen between them. Brighton wasn't interested enough to even give him a kiss when they'd been inches apart.

Tanner moved away from the door and finished cleaning up in the barn. Then he wandered around outside, checking that there wasn't any damage. Thankfully, the tree that had come down hadn't been too close to the barn. It looked closer than it had been during the storm, and Tanner added the cleanup to the list of things he needed to complete. At least he wasn't likely to run out of chores anytime soon. Now it was just a matter of how long Brighton wanted to keep him on. The farm wasn't bringing in any money, so he figured it wouldn't be very long before he'd be trying to find a job again. He returned to the barn and decided it was time to finish up for the day. Clouds were rolling in again, and it looked like more rain was on the way.

"See you tomorrow," Tanner said as he climbed the porch steps.

Brighton looked up from the computer on his lap. He'd been completely engrossed in what he was doing. "Yes. I appreciate all your help." Brighton placed the computer to the side and used the cane to get to his feet. "You're a good worker...."

Here it came. Tanner shifted his gaze to the ground. He knew that look. It was the same one the foreman had given him before booting him off the ranch. Tanner waited, but he didn't hear anything else. Tanner lifted his gaze to see what was wrong and what had stopped the inevitable. Brighton stared at him, mouth open, midword. "It's okay. I know I'm a dummy and...."

The sound of Brighton's cane clattering on the wooden porch floor startled him. Brighton moved closer, and Tanner saw him swallow hard. Was Brighton going to kiss him? His heart raced at the thought.

"You're not a dummy," Brighton whispered. "And I don't want you talking that way. I'll see you tomorrow."

Tanner stepped back. "Okay." He bent down, picked up Brighton's cane, and handed it to him. His hat tumbled from his head, and he plopped it back on with more force than necessary.

Then he turned and walked to his bike, which he'd parked just inside the garage door. He didn't understand Brighton. It was obvious that they had come close to kissing—twice—but Brighton kept stopping. Tanner wished he had someone he could talk to, he really did. But he didn't talk a lot to anyone. Maybe he'd figure it out eventually. Or maybe he'd simply do the best work he could because he needed the job and stay away from any other entanglements, no matter how much the thought of Brighton lying under him, eyes shining, without a hint of the pain that was always in them, made his blood race and his jeans way too damned tight.

Tanner started the engine and rode home just ahead of the rain. He got his bike in the garage and closed the door as the rain started again. Instead of going in the house, he went right up to his room and cleaned up. What he needed was time alone to think. But there were no real answers. After he'd cleaned up, he figured he should get dinner. The small storm had already blown through, so he was about to get on his bike when Alicia opened the back door and called him to the house for dinner. Tanner did as she asked. The house was quiet.

"The boys are at my mother's for the night," she explained. "Arthur should be home soon." She began fixing him a plate.

"Do you hate me?" Tanner asked. Sometimes some of the bluntness he'd seen the other men use out West was helpful. He wasn't sure, but her continued aloofness bothered him.

She stopped still. "No." She finished fixing the plate and put it in front of him. "I don't really know you. The boys love you because you play with them, but you never say anything and... I thought you didn't like me."

Tanner rubbed the back of his neck nervously. "I d... d... don't talk much."

"I've noticed your stutter." She got a beer and placed it next to him. "You know that doesn't matter. The boys love you, but they ask why Uncle Tanner doesn't talk." She sat in the chair across from him. "It doesn't matter to them either."

"It matters to me," he said.

"But it shouldn't." She smiled. "Arthur told me what happened back in Montana, and I wanted to say that you're welcome here. You're family, and you should be happy. They were jerks and shouldn't treat you that way just because you're gay."

"I th… thought… maybe you were like them."

"I understand that it's part of who you are. You can't change it. Love is love as far as I'm concerned." She smiled, and some of the uncertainty that had swirled around him for months began to settle. "Is there someone you like?"

"I guess. B… b… but he doesn't like me. I don't think." This was so hard to talk about. His stutter got worse, and the words caught in his throat.

"Did you talk to him?" Alicia asked and then rolled her eyes. "Of course you didn't. You're a man and don't talk about things like that."

"I only m… met him yesterday."

"Your boss? The guy at the farm?"

Tanner nodded. "He's very nice, and he almost kissed me, but I don't think he likes me that way." The words tumbled out fast before he could stop them.

She cradled her glass in her hands. "Or maybe he isn't sure you like *him* that way." Tanner opened his mouth in surprise and closed it again. "Maybe he isn't interested or maybe he isn't sure you're interested in him. Doesn't he use a cane or something?"

Tanner nodded. "He hurts a lot. He sat and talked with me today while I worked."

Alicia shook her head. "You men. You don't get women *or* each other."

"What do I do?" Tanner asked.

"Do you like him? I mean, really like him?" Tanner nodded. "Then do what men have done for centuries. Ask him out on a date."

Tanner liked that idea. He'd have to wait until after the funeral, but knowing what he wanted to do made him feel better. "Thank you," he told her and then smiled as he ate. "You're very nice." He got a smile in return.

CHAPTER 3

BRIGHTON WAS getting ready for his grandfather's funeral. He'd quickly come to rely on Tanner for a lot of things, and it scared the fuck out of him. Not being able to drive really sucked, and Brianne being busy made it even more difficult. Thankfully he had the truck. With Tanner's help Brighton had moved his few things out of his apartment and given his notice. At least that would reduce his expenses, and what he had been paying in rent could now be used to cover the utilities at the farm. But he had to figure out how to make the farm pay if it was going to survive, especially since he'd just found the tax bill for the property on his grandfather's desk. He had the money to pay it because of what Grandpa had left him, but that bill would make quite a dent in what he had. Brighton pushed all that aside. Brianne was going to be picking him up soon, and he needed to be ready.

"Brighton," Tanner called up the stairs.

He threw his tie and jacket over his shoulder, picked up his cane, and walked to the stairs. "Hey, Tanner." He felt miserable and knew he looked even worse. "What do you need?"

"I was j… j… just checking." Tanner turned away.

Brighton sighed. Tanner was huge, but he took every question as an accusation, and then he would stutter his answers. At other times his speech was clear and clean as could be. "I'm okay." He just needed to get down these stairs in one piece and then through this memorial service, funeral, whatever anyone wanted to call it. Tanner hurried up the stairs and took his arm, helping him get down. He'd already fallen once this week and was lucky the only things he'd hurt were his pride and his ass. As he reached the bottom of the stairs his phone rang. It was Brianne.

"Brighton, my car died. I'm in it, and it won't start at all. I don't know what to do."

He sighed and looked at Tanner. "Just a minute." He covered the phone. "Brianne's car won't start, and she needs a ride. I can't drive, so I was wondering if—" Brighton stopped. "No. I'll call a taxi, and we can get there that way. It—"

"I'll drive you," Tanner said. "Do you mind if I stay for the funeral? I could come back here, but then I'd just have to go right back."

"Tanner is going to take us," Brighton told Brianne. "We'll need to stop at his place so he can change, and then we'll be by to pick you up. The chapel is closest to you anyway." He checked his watch, thankful that they weren't cutting it too close.

"All right. I'll look for you." She hung up, and Brighton got the last of his things together.

"Thank you, Tanner." This was just one more way Tanner had been there to help him. "I hate not being able to drive. It makes me so helpless." Tanner waited for him to get ready, and after locking the door, they got in the truck.

Brighton tried to get comfortable. His leg ached something fierce. He knew it was tension because he was sure his aunt was going to make some sort of scene. A gathering with the whole family there was too good a chance for her to pass up. Tanner drove quickly but competently and a few minutes later pulled into the driveway of a very nice house. A woman stepped out.

Tanner got out. "I'll explain things," Brighton said as he rolled down his window. Tanner rushed inside, and the woman walked around to where he waited. "Hi. I'm Brighton."

"Alicia Granger."

"Arthur's wife," he said with a smile and extended his hand through the open window.

"Yes."

"My sister's car won't start, so Tanner is pitching in as driver. We need to get to my grandfather's funeral, and I can't drive." He felt like a doofus.

"Tanner's a good man," she said with a smile. "Are things working out for you?"

"Yes. We're getting the farm together, I guess. The hard part is figuring out what to do with the place." He smiled and tried not to let on that that was the biggest worry of all.

Two young boys came out of the front door and hurried up to their mother. "These are Marky and Josh. Can you say hello to Brighton? Uncle Tanner works at his farm."

"Hello," Marky said a little shyly. "Do you have aminals?" He mixed up the sounds in the word just like Brighton used to.

"I have sheep, some goats, and a pony. They're all very friendly. There used to be chickens too, but we don't have any of those anymore." Thank goodness. He had hated the things as a kid.

"Can we pet them?" Marky asked with a bright smile, bouncing slightly, and Josh nodded but didn't say anything.

"Of course." Brighton lifted his gaze. "Maybe your mom could bring you out sometime. You could pet the goats and sheep and ride the pony." He smiled at Alicia.

"We wouldn't want to impose."

"It would be great. When I was about Marky's age, I had a lamb that followed me around everywhere when I'd visit. It didn't hurt that I had treats and spoiled him rotten. They really are friendly, and you'd be welcome."

Tanner came out in dress pants and a white shirt. He looked nice. Alicia backed the boys away from the truck, explaining that they had to go. Tanner called out to both boys and waved good-bye.

THEY MADE it to the chapel with five minutes to spare. Tanner dropped Brighton and Brianne off at the front door and then parked. The chapel looked nice with some flowers and the remains in a bronze box on a stand surrounded by bouquets. It was elegant and pretty. "Thank you. It looks nice," Brighton told his aunt as he peered around.

She smiled a little. "You do what you have to." Aunt Vera wiped her eyes and looked toward the front of the chapel, sniffing lightly.

Brighton thought that a really weird response, but then he didn't put anything past her. He truly hoped she was broken up by her father's passing. Brianne hugged her, and then Brighton did the same, silently chastising himself for trying to see ulterior motives in someone at a time like this. "I appreciate it, and it looks lovely. The colors are perfect."

She nodded, and Brighton stepped back and off to the side. Tanner came in and joined them. Brighton saw Aunt Vera look at them, probably wondering who Tanner was, but other people arrived, and she went off to greet them, handkerchief in hand. Uncle Raymond stood off to the side talking to his sons, Mick and Tim, as well as his daughter, Jill. Brighton's three cousins looked toward him with scowls on their faces. Uncle Raymond was the one to offer a slight smile and walked over to say hello. "Sorry about that business at the farm," he said softly. Brighton had already figured Aunt Vera was behind all that anyway. "Your aunt gets a bee in her bonnet and…."

Brighton nodded. If there was one person in the family he felt for, it was his uncle. He spent much of his life trying to make Aunt Vera happy—a monumental task if there ever was one. "It's all right. Emotions were running high, and I'm sure things will settle down."

His aunt signaled, and Uncle Raymond sighed softly before moving away. "Don't count on it."

Brighton turned to Brianne, wondering what that was about. He shifted his gaze to his cousins, but the three of them had their heads together—never a good sign. It certainly hadn't been when he and Brianne had lived with their aunt and uncle. Thank goodness that had been a brief period in their lives. "Don't let them get to you," Brianne said. "We're here to say good-bye to Grandpa."

Brighton nodded and slowly walked toward the front, where all that was left of his grandfather, the only person other than Brianne who'd truly loved him, sat in a bronze box.

Tanner gently touched his arm, and when Brighton turned to him, Tanner simply smiled and patted his arm. "It's okay," he said.

Brighton continued forward with Brianne on one side and Tanner on the other. His legs felt like lead, and he had to force them to move. Truth be known, he hated that his grandfather had been cremated, but there was nothing he could do about it now, and it had been what his grandfather had wanted. He would just have liked the opportunity to look down at him one last time to say a final good-bye.

Brianne stepped forward first, and Brighton leaned on Tanner so he didn't fall. He was so steady and strong. Damn, he'd known Tanner less than a week, and he was standing beside him at his grandfather's funeral. He remembered the last funeral he'd gone to. It had been the one for their parents. God, the fear that had welled inside him that day, not knowing what was going to happen to him and Brianne, losing the people who had always been there and taken care of them. His mom and dad were the best. They had listened and never yelled, even when things went bad. Brighton breathed deeply to try to dispel the sadness of that day. It was long ago. He hadn't expected all that to come up, but it mixed with the current loss and left Brighton feeling the weight of the world settle on his shoulders. Brianne stepped back, and Brighton held out his hand. She grasped it and squeezed lightly.

"Go on and say hello to people," Brighton said. "I just need a minute."

"Are you sure?" Brianne asked.

"Yeah," he said. Brianne squeezed his hand once again and then released it. "Maybe you can see if the entire family thinks I'm the Grinch."

Brianne let go of his hand and hugged him. "Most don't care, and the others don't like Vera much anyway." Brighton hugged her in return, and then she released him. She smiled and moved off. Brighton stepped closer and stared at the box.

Tanner released his arm and stepped back but didn't go too far.

"Are you his keeper?" Brighton heard Tim snicker just within hearing range.

"No," Tanner said deeply, with a hint of menace. He might be a man of few words, but Tanner seemed to be able to make the ones he said count.

Brighton used his cane for balance and stepped closer to the bronze box on the stand. "It seems dumb to be talking to a box instead of you," Brighton whispered under his breath. He didn't want anyone to hear him. "I wish you were here so I could ask you what you want me to do. I feel like you asked me to carry on your legacy, and I'm trying, but I'm lost." Brighton swallowed around the grapefruit that formed in his throat. "I feel you in the house all the time and expect to see you in your chair on the porch or wandering through the barn." Brighton took a deep breath. "All the animals seem to miss you. Hell...." Brighton wiped his eyes with the back of his hand. "I miss you." Brighton tried to hold back the wave of loneliness that washed over him.

Tanner lightly touched his arm, and Brighton moved instinctively toward his touch. It was so gentle and kind. "It will be okay," Tanner whispered.

Brighton wasn't sure he believed that. "I wish I had come to see you more, especially these last few years. I wish I'd really gotten to know you as an adult instead of just as your grandson." He had so many regrets where his grandpa was concerned. Brighton sniffed and stood as straight as he could. "I'll do my best to make you proud."

Brighton turned, and Tanner helped him walk away from the bronze box. Brighton let Tanner guide him to a seat in front and then sat next to him. He was glad Tanner had come with him. "Thank you. I'm sorry I'm wasting your time."

Tanner just shook his head and looked around. Brighton wished the service would start.

"Have you decided what you're going to do?" Jill asked as she took the seat on the other side of Tanner. "The farm is a lot of work. Even Grandpa said that."

"I know. But it was his desire that someone try to carry it on, and he chose me. I wish I knew what he was thinking," Brighton said.

"Maybe he wasn't. Toward the end he wasn't really thinking very clearly sometimes. Maybe he was confused or—"

"Stop it, Jill. He wasn't confused. Grandpa knew what he wanted and always did. You know that." He also saw through the game Jill was playing. At home she had always picked and picked until Brighton had had enough. Then she'd run and tell her mother that Brighton was being mean to her. "He certainly saw through your games." He smiled and watched as her false smile faded and curled into the grimace she usually wore. "I always thought you'd be happier if you just accepted what you had instead of worrying about everyone else. I don't have any more than you do. I live simply."

She paused for a second, her features softening for a few seconds. "But your simple life is affecting the rest of us. You should just sell the farm."

Brighton shook his head. "It doesn't matter what you think. That farm is all we have left of Grandpa. He's in a stupid box. So as long as the farm is alive in those animals and the other things, then he'll live." He hadn't realized that was how he felt until the words crossed his lips. "Think of it this way, Jill. I'm keeping the farm alive and going not just for me, but for the next generation. If I can make it work, then it will be there for your children or Mick's or Tim's. If we sell it, then it's gone. Grandpa knew that."

Her scowl returned, and Jill stood. "I knew you wouldn't get it."

Brighton sighed and turned away from her as she walked away. It didn't really matter. He now had a vision of why he needed to save the farm. He simply had to figure out a way to make it happen.

The minister walked through the crowd and went to stand near the front. He didn't say anything right away, and everyone in the room found their seats. Brianne sat in the chair Jill had vacated. Brighton stared at the minister, a middle-aged man he didn't know from Adam. But he had a kind face that wore a soft expression like a comfortable old sweatshirt.

"Good afternoon. We're here to say good-bye to a friend, parent, and grandparent." He smiled just a little. "Edward touched the life of every one of us in some way. So what I'd like to do, rather than me giving a third-party eulogy, is allow each of you to come forward and say how Edward touched your life." He paused. "Edward was the first one who believed in me. See, I wanted to follow my calling and become a minister. My parents, while happy with my decision, really wanted me to go into finance or something with a lot more earning potential." He smiled. "I'm not telling you this to belittle them. We didn't have much, and they wanted me to have a better life than they'd had. Edward went with me to explain what I wanted to do. He stood behind me. Turns out I didn't need it. My parents respected my decision, but I wasn't alone. And that's what I'll never forget. Not being alone."

He stepped aside and waited a few seconds. No one got up. Brighton peered around, hoping someone would step forward. Brianne stood up next to him and walked forward. "I'm Brianne, Edward's granddaughter. My parents were killed when I was fourteen. My brother and I went to live with our aunt and uncle." Her gaze shifted. "It was a hard time for me. I wasn't a very pleasant person. Life wasn't fair, and I hated everyone and everything. The world had somehow conspired to take away those I loved most." Brianne paused. "I appreciate what everyone did for Brighton and me at that time. But it was Grandpa who told me that life went on. He held me and told me that I needed to be strong and make my own way. He said I'd have help but that I was smart and funny, and I could move the world if I put my mind to it." She turned to the minister and nodded. "Like you, I never had to worry that I was alone. Grandpa always seemed to have my back. Most of the time I didn't even realize he was there."

Brighton nodded when he caught Brianne's gaze. He felt much the same way and was pleased as Brianne sat back down. There was no need to go into old hurts. Grandpa had been there for both of them, especially when things had gotten very difficult for them living with their aunt, uncle, and cousins.

Brianne's story seemed to have broken the ice. Others got up. One man told about the time Grandpa got bucked in the rear end by one of the goats. One of the ladies talked about how she had been trying to get their grandmother's recipe for clam chowder for years. She laughed. "I'll never forget the day I went over to ask Ed for the recipe, and he just handed me a can of chowder with that mischievous smile he always had. He said Eleanor had sworn him to secrecy, but now that she was gone...." She took a handkerchief out of her purse. "The old coot."

Brighton couldn't help smiling. He could see his grandfather doing just that.

"There was always a zest for life around Eddie," a huge, gray-haired man said as he took the woman's place. He didn't move fast, but there was power in him nonetheless. "I'm Thaddeus Winters, and Eddie and I were kids together. Our farm was right next to the one Eddie lived on his entire life. He and I would terrorize the cows and torment the goats. Our mothers used to scold us, saying we were going to turn the milk sour." He stopped to smile. "When we grew up, Eddie married my cousin, and these young ones in front are part of my family." He motioned to all of them. "They don't know me because I moved to California after my folks sold the farm. But Eddie fought the good fight. He kept the farm going all those years. The land I grew up on and played on is now a mini-mall. I can't recognize anything except Eddie's place."

Thaddeus wiped his eyes briefly. "I haven't seen my childhood friend in a lot of years, but we used to write and talk on the phone. Up until the end, he was the same Eddie I remembered, full of life." He paused again, and Brighton could see how hard this was for him. He'd been on the edge of tears for a long time himself. Brighton stood slowly and walked to where his relative, one he'd never met, stood up in front, floundering in his loss. "My last friend, of the ones you make when friends really mean something, is gone." Brighton took his arm, and his distant cousin seemed to rally his thoughts. "We always like to think things were simpler back then, and maybe they were. I don't know. Kids today have all the conveniences, but I'd like to think that things are just as simple, friends are still as magical, and they get into the same kinds of mischief and have the same adventures that Eddie and I had." He wiped his eyes and moved to sit back down, lightly touching Brighton's hand as he did.

Brighton forced a smile and turned to the collected group. "I want to share a favorite memory. I was turning ten. Mom had baked a cake, and we had taken it over to Grandma and Grandpa's because it was my birthday, and I had asked to have my party at the farm." Brighton inhaled deeply. "See, I figured if it was there, I'd get extra presents." Brighton shrugged as people smiled and chuckled softly. "I was a kid—what did I know? Anyway, when we got to the house, there were no wrapped packages in sight except the ones my parents brought. We had lunch and then cut the cake. Mom and Dad let me open my presents, and then I remember looking at Grandma." He let his gaze flow over the people. They were all watching him closely. "Grandma looked at Grandpa, and she put her hand over her mouth and gasped like she'd forgotten the present. Then she laughed and said my present was out in the barn. Did they get me a pony? I was so excited I jumped up and ran out to the barn. Grandpa followed behind, and when he caught up, he took me to a small pen and picked up a lamb. It was so small. He handed him to me along with a bottle. He told me the mother had died and that he needed someone to care for him. Grandma said they were going to give him to me and that I was going to stay with them for a few weeks to help raise him." Brighton sighed and smiled. "I practically slept in the barn for a week. I actually would have if Grandma had let me."

Many heads nodded, and there were smiles on many faces. He purposely ignored the flat expressions of his aunt and cousins. They didn't matter, at least not at that moment.

"For the longest time I thought the lamb was my present. But as it grew older, it melded into the rest of the little flock they had, and other than following me around sometimes, I had little contact with him once he grew. No, the real present wasn't the lamb—it was the time. It was the weeks I spent with Grandma and Grandpa caring for and holding that little lamb. That was the gift—caring for another living being while at the same time being cared for and having the chance to run and play and enjoy being outdoors, just like Mr. Winters said. They gave me a few weeks of the kind of childhood most children don't get. In essence, the real gift was their time and their love. And the lesson, I guess, is to make the most of it, because eventually it will end. We grow up, move on, and all we'll have are the memories." Brighton slowly returned to his seat, thankful as heck that he'd been able to say what he wanted to without completely falling to pieces.

He got to his chair and sat down. Brianne handed him a tissue and shared a quick smile with him. He turned to Tanner, who leaned closer. "Th... that was real nice." Others got up and spoke, taking a few minutes to tell what his grandfather meant to them. Finally, his aunt got up, and she spent some time talking about growing up with her father. It sounded rehearsed and dry. Once she sat down, the minister came up again and said a few closing words, and then the gathering broke up.

Lunch was being served, so they made their way to the restaurant, a short distance away. It wasn't anything fancy, but Grandpa had been a breakfast regular there for a number of years, so it seemed fitting. The people tended to split off into groups based upon who knew whom. Brighton sat with Brianne and Tanner at the end of a larger table that remained otherwise empty until Mr. Winters sat down across the table, next to Brianne. "Is it okay to join you?"

"Of course," Brianne said brightly. "Our other relatives aren't particularly pleased with us right now."

He made a derisive sound, and Brighton grew to like him immediately. "Apparently there's some sort of fight going on over the farm."

"Not at all. Grandpa left it to me, and I'm going to live there, at least for a while." He shifted slightly. "This is Tanner. He's helping me at the farm. I can't drive, and any sort of heavy work is out of the question, so he's been doing most of the chores."

68

Mr. Winters extended his hand, and Tanner shook it. "You look like you were made for farm work."

"I was on a r... ranch before I m... m... moved here." Tanner stopped.

Mr. Winters nodded toward the other family members. "So I take it they think you should sell? What skin is it off their nose anyhow what you do with what's yours?"

"If I sell, they get part of the money. If I stay, then the farm is mine." Brighton glanced over as his three cousins huddled their heads together. "I understand what Grandpa was doing, but it's created a lot of problems. Not that we were particularly close to begin with, but Aunt Vera was counting on the sale of the farm to help finance the lifestyle to which she'd like to become accustomed."

Mr. Winters made his derisive sound again. "You stick to your guns."

"I intend to, provided I can figure out how to make the farm pay. You've seen the place. It's surrounded by development on all sides, and it really isn't that big."

"You need to take lemons and make lemonade. The land is good. It always has been. So figure out what people around you need and provide it. Vegetables always work. You could grow a bunch and sell them at a stand. Raise animals for meat." He paused. "Though the smell can be a bit overpowering, and you want to be a good neighbor."

"You understand my problem. I've got fifty acres. I could plant it in corn and make next to nothing."

"True. But there is that orchard area. Fruit trees can pay. Especially in an area like yours, when you can offer fresh-picked or let folks pick their own."

"True, but the trees are really old, and it would take years to grow new ones," Brighton said.

Mr. Winters rolled his eyes. "Son, you're just a barrel of sunshine, aren't you? You need to figure out what you *can* do. You've got a barn, so you can keep critters. You got some land, so you can grow stuff. Figure out what will make the most of all of it and do that. You work otherwise, right?"

"Yes."

"So all you've got to get is enough to make the land support itself. It will do that pretty much on its own if you let it." Mr. Winters turned to Tanner. "You got any ideas, son? I see you listening. I bet you got something." Tanner shrugged. "If you got something to say...."

"I k... keep thinking about the s... story Brighton told about baby animals. Everyone loves baby animals."

"They do," Brighton admitted. "But how do we make that into a business?"

"That's what you gotta figure out." Mr. Winters smiled as the server set plates in front of each of them. "There are websites about nothing but baby animals."

"Okay," Brighton said, mostly to get off the subject. He wanted to figure out what he was going to do with the farm, but somehow he didn't think now was the best time to brainstorm business ideas. "We'll have to give it some thought." Brighton took a bite of his ham. "How long are you staying in town?"

"I'm here until tomorrow. I'm staying with some friends. I have a flight first thing."

"If you have time, please stop by the farm."

"I'll try, but if I can't this time, I'll surely do that the next time I'm in the area." He smiled and began to eat.

The conversation dropped off, and they ate their lunches. Once folks finished eating, there was a lot more mingling, and people joined them at their table, sharing stories about their grandfather. It was a pleasant enough afternoon.

"We need to get back," Brighton told Brianne when Tanner pointed to his watch. "The critters need to be fed, and Tanner needs to go home." He stood and said good-bye to everyone at the table. Brighton then found Mr. Winters and said a special good-bye to him, reiterating his invitation to come visit.

"I will," Mr. Winters said with a smile. After saying their farewells to everyone, they headed out to the truck. Tanner said good-bye to Brianne and finalized their plans for graduation, Brighton insisted that he was taking Brianne out for a celebration dinner afterward, and then they headed back to the farm. When they arrive, Brighton went inside to get some work done, and Tanner walked to the barn. "Shouldn't you change?" Brighton asked, holding the door open.

Tanner got a bag out of his truck and followed him inside. Once he'd changed he went right out to the barn, and Brighton got his computer and sat in his favorite chair. After a while Tanner came out of the barn and closed the door for the night. He walked over to where Brighton sat. "I'm g... going."

Brighton set his computer aside and stood. "Thank you for everything today. You were a lifesaver, and you didn't need to do all that." He tried to remember the last time someone other than Brianne had done something for him simply to be kind, and he had a hard time... other than Grandpa. Brighton stepped closer, intending to pat Tanner on the shoulder, but his leg gave out, and he fell forward. Tanner caught him in his strong arms, pressing Brighton to his massive chest. Brighton lifted his gaze to meet Tanner's, and then Tanner kissed him.

Tanner's lips on his sent jolts of energy though his entire body. His eyes slid closed. This was what he'd dreamed of. Excitement rose quickly, and Brighton shifted, unsure if Tanner wanted to feel just how much he was affected. Then Tanner's hold increased as he slipped one hand down onto his butt, half holding him up, while he wrapped the other tightly around Brighton's back, pressing him to Tanner's brick-wall chest. Tanner devoured his mouth. Brighton moaned softly, letting go of the cane. It fell to the porch floor, but Brighton didn't care. He pressed his hands to Tanner's powerful chest and then slid them up and around his neck, where he held on for dear life.

When the kiss broke, Brighton gasped for air and caught Tanner's heated gaze for a split second, and then Tanner slanted his lips over Brighton's once more. God, Tanner tasted good, felt good—hell, he even sounded good with that rich rumbling moan from deep in his throat. Brighton's feet left the porch floor as Tanner moved them toward the house. Brighton held on, not daring to break the kiss, needing the energy Tanner was pouring into him, soaking it in like a sponge.

Tanner got the door open, and the screen banged closed once they'd passed inside. The wall pressed against Brighton's back, and Tanner's firm, welcome weight anchored his front. Tanner lowered Brighton back onto his feet, their lips offsetting slightly. Brighton flexed his hip, and his encased erection found Tanner's equally sizable one pressing right back.

"Tanner," Brighton whispered, raising his chin as Tanner slid his tongue down his neck. The word trailed off in a whimper. He couldn't hold his own weight. Between his bad leg and what Tanner was doing to him, if he moved away, he would slide down the wall to the floor. But he trusted Tanner and knew that wouldn't happen. Tanner kissed Brighton again, this time a little more gently, and then the pressure lightened and came to an end. "Damn."

"I w... wanted to...."

Brighton could feel nervousness radiating out from Tanner, replacing the flow of positive energy with something darker. Brighton pulled Tanner forward, kissing him to cut off the words. They weren't needed. They had done plenty of talking without the need for words in the last few seconds, and Brighton was more than ready to continue that particular conversation.

When Tanner pulled away this time, though, it was with a heated smile. He gently stroked Brighton's cheek. Tanner's hard cock throbbed next to his, and Brighton closed his eyes, relishing the feel of something he hadn't expected to feel again... well, other than his own. "I should probably go," Tanner whispered without a hint of the stutter. The nerves seemed to have subsided, but Brighton wasn't sure. Tanner backed away slightly. Brighton used the wall to make sure he was steady on his feet. Then Tanner moved away completely.

Even in the warm air, Brighton was slightly chilled by the absence of Tanner's intense heat. Tanner left the room, then returned with Brighton's cane, which he pressed into his hand. "See you tomorrow."

Brighton nodded, a little dazed by what had happened. He blinked a few times and watched Tanner leave the room, the screen door banging behind him. Damn, he'd never been kissed like that before. Sure, Brighton had had men kiss him—he'd had boyfriends. Well, *a* boyfriend, but in the time they were together, none of their kisses had melted Brighton's shoes the way those kisses from Tanner had. When he looked down, he half expected bare feet and a black ooze on the carpet.

He took a deep breath and got his cane in place before daring to take a single step away from the supportive wall. His heart still pounded as the throaty rumble of Tanner's motorcycle broke the quiet. Brighton peered out the window and watched Tanner ride away. That sight seemed to pierce the spell he'd been under.

Brighton sighed and let the old curtain fall back into place. Tanner was strong, vibrant, intense, and, Jesus... hot enough to melt lead. So what in the hell could he see in a man whose leg gave out at odd times, who couldn't even walk across the yard without help? Those kisses aside, what in the hell could Tanner see in him? Brighton wasn't a whole man, and Tanner deserved so much more than him. He turned and slowly made his way to the kitchen. He was still full from lunch but really thirsty. He pulled open the refrigerator door and pulled out a beer. Hell, he grabbed two bottles, holding them between his fingers. The rough edges of the bottle caps dug into his fingers a little, but he didn't care. Brighton pushed the refrigerator door closed and then left the room, returned to the porch, and lowered himself into the chair. He dropped the cane next to him, popped open the first beer, and drank half of it in a single pull.

He needed something. Every doubt he'd felt for months, everything he'd questioned about his life, came rushing at him all at once. He needed to drown them out somehow. Two beers wasn't going to do it, but it was a grand start, and once they were gone, he could move on to something that would certainly do the trick. Brighton finished the beer and opened the next one, holding it in his hands, rocking slowly in the chair. "I miss you, Grandpa." He took a drink. "Why couldn't you have told me what you wanted me to do with this place? You left me this land, but…." For the millionth time he thought about throwing in the towel. Regardless of what he'd said at the funeral, maybe it would be best to simply sell up and get out. It would make everyone happy. Brighton sighed, knowing even as the thought rang through his head that selling wouldn't make *him* happy.

Brighton finished his beer and then stood. He was slightly wobbly on his feet but determined. He grabbed his cane and slowly descended the two steps and made his way across the yard. He opened the barn door and stepped inside.

It smelled of fresh straw, hay, and of the animals. He walked to the sheep pen and sat on the bale of straw. One of the sheep came over, and Brighton gently stroked the rough, matted wool. He remembered his lamb and how soft the wool had been. He'd need to get them sheared for the summer. There were lots of things he needed to do. "You like it here, don't you?" Brighton said, and the sheep blinked at him before wandering off again. "I do too." He wished he knew what he was going to do, and he sure as hell wished he wasn't so fucking weak.

His thoughts shifted from the farm to Tanner. What was he going to do? He'd wanted Tanner to kiss him. Hell, ever since he'd met Tanner, Brighton had wanted to climb him like Mount Everest. But what could he possibly see in Brighton? He was broken, and Tanner was so healthy. Guys like him didn't go for skinny, gimpy men. Tanner could have anyone he wanted; he just didn't know it. What if Brighton did pursue Tanner, and then he realized just what he could have? Tanner wouldn't stick with a nobody like him, that was for damn sure. "I wish I knew the answers."

One of the goats pushed her head between the slats of the pen, peering at him strangely. "That's exactly how I feel—confused and stupid." Brighton stared back. "I wish you had the answers, because I sure as hell don't." The goat just looked at him, blinking a few times. "Yeah, you're no help." Brighton got to his feet and moved to the stall where the pony munched his hay. Brighton softly petted his neck as he thought. "There has to be a way to make enough money to keep all of you in feed and straw." The bill for the delivery and supplies from earlier in the week had been an eye-opener. He hadn't expected things to be so expensive, but damn. He had some money; however, the farm would run through it pretty fast if he didn't do something to supplement it. He wondered how his grandfather had done it. Grandpa had kept the critters fed and housed all these years without going broke. Or had there been more money that Grandpa had simply used up?

Everything was out of control, and he didn't understand it. Farming was a mystery; Tanner was a bigger mystery. Brighton shifted his gaze from the pony to his legs. Maybe if he were whole, he could handle this, but he was mostly helpless in his own home. He owned the bloody farm but could do almost nothing with it himself. "Fuck, that's attractive," he groused out loud.

Brighton sat in the barn as the light through the door softened and then dimmed. Finally, before it got completely dark, he left the barn, closing the door before going back to the house. He wasn't particularly hungry, but he made something simple that he could nuke, tasting very little of it. As it got dark, he thought about watching television, but he was exhausted, emotionally and physically. He slowly climbed the stairs. His leg hurt like a son of a bitch, and he figured it was time he went back to the doctor. If things were getting worse, he needed to know.

He lived in constant fear that the things that had been done to put his leg back together would fail and he'd end up in a wheelchair or without a leg at all. He made it to the top of the stairs and caned his way to the bathroom. It was old as hell but functional. When he got around to making major improvements, this was the first room he would redo. He wanted a huge whirlpool bath so he could soak his leg. Right now that sounded like heaven. But as usual, heaven would have to wait. He used the toilet, cleaned up, and left the bathroom.

Bless Brianne's heart she had done a very nice job of setting up a bedroom for him. It was warm, inviting, and felt like home. The other rooms in the house all felt like Grandpa's. This one was his. Brighton opened the window and then got undressed, sliding between the sheets. He was warm, and the air was sticky. Brighton had to do something about air-conditioning, at least for his room.

Eventually the cooler night air permeated the room, and Brighton felt sleep approach. But his mind wouldn't turn off. All he could think about was Tanner, that kiss, and what it meant. He liked the man, hell, he was fascinated by him, and he'd sat on the porch for hours just so he could watch him. Brighton knew it might be a little stalkerish, but damn. He closed his eyes and saw Tanner bending over to set posts or lifting the heavy beams, the muscles under his shirt straining, pressing the seams to their limits.

It wasn't just Tanner's physical attributes, though there were plenty of those. He liked him and enjoyed talking with him. Sure, he didn't say a whole lot, but so what? Small talk was overrated. Meaningful conversation was what counted, and actions, and Tanner had been kind enough to take him and Brianne to the funeral. Without a doubt Tanner was a kind soul wrapped in a hunkalicious package. What Brighton couldn't figure out was what he'd want with a skinny, gimpy-legged guy like him. He really had nothing to offer, and anyway, Tanner was his employee. He sighed and tried to go to sleep, but it stayed just out of reach for hours. Somehow he had to be bright-eyed and bushy-tailed for Brianne's graduation the next day. But no matter what, he was going to do his best to make it special for her.

CHAPTER 4

TANNER ARRIVED at the house Monday morning first thing. He yawned big-time as he pulled open the barn door. All he could think about was the feel of Brighton's lips on his and the way he'd tasted. More than once he'd stood still, eyes closed, thinking of Brighton and how alive he'd felt and the way he vibrated against him when Brighton clung to him. He yawned again, wondering for a second if he needed to find a place to be alone for a few seconds. Instead he walked to the sheep pen and peered inside.

Empty. The pen was empty. Instantly, Tanner's tiredness disappeared. He shook his head to make sure he wasn't seeing things and jumped into the pen, then hurried over to the small door. It swung open. That in itself shouldn't have been an issue. Tanner stepped outside, figuring the sheep were in their outside area. To his dismay, the pen was empty. He didn't see where the fence had failed right away, but then he spotted a single board right near the barn lying on the ground. Tanner groaned and then climbed on the fence, looking around. He needed to find those four sheep. He spotted what looked like one of them on the far edge of the property. Swearing softly under his breath, Tanner took off across the field. He slowed as he saw the small group of sheep, heads down, munching on the grass.

One of them lifted its head, bleated softly, and began moving away. The others followed. Tanner walked in a large circle and came up behind them. The lead sheep turned and began leading the small flock back toward the barn. "Go on, you stupid sheep," Tanner said without heat as they continued.

As he approached the yard, Tanner saw Brighton heading to the barn. He stopped when he saw the small parade. Brighton opened the gate to the pen, and the sheep went inside. Tanner continued behind them, making sure they went all the way into the barn. He closed the door and hurried inside to secure it. "They decided to go for a walk," Tanner said, feeling like a fool for not latching the door more thoroughly. "I need to fix the fence before we can let them out again." Thankfully he had the stuff he needed.

"I'll feed if you can haul the water," Brighton said. "Then you can fix the fence."

"Thank you." Tanner filled buckets and made sure all the critters had water before hurrying outside and getting to work on the fence. It was going to be a hot one. Already the sun was beating down. Tanner pulled off his light shirt, tossed it over the fence, and got to work.

Making the repair didn't take long, and then he returned to the barn. "What happened?" Tanner asked, hurrying to Brighton, who was trying to get back on his feet. He caught Brighton under his arms and helped him to his feet. "D... did your knee give out?"

"No. I slipped on some straw." Brighton stood and leaned on his cane, breathing heavily. "I can't seem to do anything. I should be able to give the sheep some hay, but no." He leaned against the railing of one of the pens. "Now my leg aches, and...." Tanner lifted Brighton off his feet and swept him into his arms. "What are you doing?"

"T... taking you back to the p... porch," Tanner said, walking across the yard. He was shocked at how little Brighton weighed.

"I'm fine," Brighton protested, but Tanner didn't feel him fight at all. Instead, he settled against him and lightly stroked Tanner's chest with the hand he wasn't using to hold his cane. Heat spread from where Brighton rested his hand, radiating through his entire body. Instantly, he was hard as stone, his cock throbbing in his pants. He climbed the porch steps and gently laid Brighton on the old wicker settee.

"You need to be more careful," Tanner said in a very measured tone. He didn't want to stutter, not with Brighton's lips right there, and he could feel the nerves rising up.

"I didn't fall on purpose," Brighton said a little heatedly.

Tanner hadn't thought he had, and he opened his mouth to protest, but he knew all that would come out were sputters and bits of words, so he closed his mouth and leaned closer, kissing Brighton hard. That was the one way he knew he could quiet him, but it had the opposite effect. Brighton moaned softly and then slid an arm around Tanner's neck. He put his other hand flat on Tanner's chest, moving slightly, bumping his fingers gently over his nipple. Fuck, that felt good. Tanner deepened the kiss, wishing he hadn't stopped at the porch but instead had taken Brighton inside—hell, maybe all the way upstairs to his bed.

He pulled back and straightened up, and Brighton's hands slipped away from him. Tanner sighed and took a single step back. If they continued, he wouldn't be responsible for his actions.

"Why did you stop?" Brighton slowly sat up.

"I…." Tanner tried to think of the words. "Things don't go well for me." That was the understatement of the century.

"Me neither," Brighton said. "I have crap luck with men."

Tanner smiled. "Me t… too."

Brighton locked on to Tanner's gaze as though he was expecting Tanner to tell him about it. The thought filled him with fear. He was not proud of what had happened. "I gotta…," he began and then pointed toward the barn. Then he turned and hurried off the porch and back across the yard. In the barn, he put the goats out into their pen and began cleaning the stall. He needed physical work, something to work these feelings out of his system. They had to go. He could not go through what he had before. Not that he thought Brighton was like Royce and his family—just thinking about them made his blood boil.

"Uncle Tanner?" He turned, delighted and surprised, as his nephew ran into the barn. Marky stopped and held his nose. "PU," he said. "There's poop in here." He went up on his tiptoes. "Is that the poop?"

Tanner was shook his head at his nephew's reaction. "It's goat poop." He couldn't help smiling. He didn't smell stuff like that much anymore. "Let me empty this, and I can show you and Josh the animals."

"But no poop," Marky said, then turned and left the barn. Tanner finished up and took the last load of muck out. Alicia and the two boys stood outside of the paddock where the pony munched on grass, paying little attention to any of them. Tanner emptied the wheelbarrow and then approached the small group.

"I'm glad you came."

"Brighton said we could stop by to see the animals, and the boys were so full of energy I had to get them out of the house." Alicia looked frazzled.

"I need to finish. Th... then I'll be right back." Tanner hurried back inside and spread new bedding in the pen. Then he returned, lifting Marky in the air to squeals of delight. "Th... those are goats." Tanner pulled open the gate and took Josh by the hand, leading him inside. The goats gathered around curiously.

"Do they bite?" Marky asked.

"Only if they feel threatened."

Marky petted one of the goats. Josh hung back for a while until Marky began to laugh. Alicia watched from the fence. Eventually Josh petted one of the goats and then turned to his mom with a grin. "Hairy."

"Yes, they're hairy," Alicia agreed. Josh turned back and gently petted the goat again. There were only four of them, but they all jostled for the boys' attention.

He watched the boys, and when he turned back to where Alicia stood, Brighton had joined her. They were talking, and Brighton watched the boys with a smile.

"Uncle Tanner, can we ride the pony?" Marky asked, pointing toward the paddock.

Tanner turned to Brighton, who nodded. "Of course. There's a saddle in the barn."

Tanner got it, along with the brushes and comb. When he returned, he lifted the boys away from the goats and entered the paddock. He groomed the pony and then saddled him before leading him out into the yard. "What's the pony's name?" Marky asked Brighton.

"Napoleon," Brighton answered, still standing next to Alicia, who took Josh's hand as Tanner lifted Marky onto the pony.

"You'll get your turn," Alicia told Josh when he fussed.

Tanner led Napoleon around the yard. Marky laughed and told Napoleon to giddyup, which the pony ignored, and they made an uneventful trip around the yard. Then Tanner helped him down and put Josh on his back. Alicia held Josh's hand, and they slowly made a circuit of the yard. Both boys seemed to love their ride, and Tanner spent the next hour walking the boys around the yard.

"Giddyup, 'Poleon," Josh yelled giddily as Tanner led the pony back up to the paddock. The pony was definitely getting tired. Tanner lifted Josh off and set him on his feet. Both boys begged for another ride.

"Uncle Tanner needs to give Napoleon a rest. But you can see the sheep now if you like," Brighton said and motioned the boys toward the pen. Marky climbed up on the fence, peering over at the huge balls of fur.

"What did you have planned for today?" Brighton asked Tanner.

"Shearing," Tanner answered, and Brighton nodded before turning to the boys. "Do you wanna watch Uncle Tanner give the sheep a haircut?" They bounced up and down, and Tanner nodded. He went in the barn and got the clippers. Shearing was a dusty business, so he figured it was best done outside. Places with lots of sheep had shearing sheds, but he'd have to make do. Tanner shooed three of the sheep inside and held the remaining animal still as he began the process of giving him a haircut.

The damn sheep bleated as though he were killing the poor thing. Of course, he wouldn't hurt it at all. He started near the head and sheared evenly down the body.

"Is Uncle Tanner hurting him?" Josh asked.

"No. The sheep just doesn't like having his hair cut any more than you do," Alicia told him, and Tanner looked at her, catching a happy smile. When he was done, Tanner released the sheep, and he raced off to the far edge of the pen. Tanner put the fleece to the side and got the next sheep.

He hadn't sheared sheep very often. The ranch had had a small flock that the missus raised for wool. She was always knitting something, and according to rumor liked to use her own wool, so the job of shearing the sheep had fallen to Tanner the last year he worked on the ranch. He'd helped the year before, but when the guy who usually did the shearing left, it had fallen to him. The boss had been too cheap to hire a professional.

Tanner sheared the other sheep, taking his time. Guys who did this for a living could shear one of these sheep in a minute flat, but Tanner wanted to do it carefully. Still, soon the sheep were clipped and back to running around the pen. "Are they cold?" Josh asked.

All eyes shifted to Tanner. "No."

"Tanner is going to make wool blankets for them," Brighton said, winking at the boys, who stared up at him like they wondered if he was telling the truth. Alicia laughed, and Tanner rolled his eyes. "That's why we shear them in summer, so they have time to grow more hair before winter."

Tanner was covered in dust and sweat. Everything the wool had picked up all year had streaked his chest and arms.

"Can you do it again?" Marky asked, looking around as if he expected to see more sheep.

"That's all th… there are," Tanner said. He pulled off his hat and wiped his brow with the back of his hand. It was getting hot already.

"I need to take the boys home, but thank you for everything." Alicia turned to the boys. "Did you have fun?"

"Thank you, Uncle Tanner," Marky said.

"Fank you," Josh added with a smile.

"I need to get them out of the sun for a while. But thank you both. They had a great time, and it was nice for them to be able to see farm animals up close. So far it's only been pictures in books." She herded the boys toward her car. Tanner grabbed his shirt and managed to get it on over his sweaty skin. Then he headed to the car, where Brighton was saying good-bye to Alicia and the boys.

Shouts of good-bye and waves were exchanged as the car turned around and then headed out the driveway.

"They had a good time. It's—" Brighton stopped and turned all the way around. "I think I have it."

"Have what?" Tanner asked.

"I think I know what I'm going to do with this place. I think we'll turn it into a petting farm."

Tanner took a step back. "A wh… what?"

"A farm for children. Sort of like what we did today. We'll have a goat pen where kids can pet and feed them. A sheep area. We can even have a few cows. Not many." Brighton practically shook with excitement. "God, I don't want chickens, but maybe rabbits, a few pigs with piglets. A place where families can come, bring their kids, and get close to animals most city kids never see for real. We could turn part of the open land into a pumpkin patch, and another part into a… I don't know, but we can figure it out."

"The orchard?" Tanner asked. "Haunted, maybe?"

Brighton grinned. "Those trees are so old and gnarled that might work, especially in the fall. We could leave part of it, and plant some new trees. In a few years, people could pick their own fruit if they wanted. We'd have to have more than the barn we have now. We could start with that but add some more. We'd need to get a few more ponies so we could give rides. The kids would love that." Brighton paused. "I've been trying to think of a way we could use the farm within its current location, and this might just work. It would help the place fit into the surroundings and make it part of the area instead of being the last hold-out to progress, or what most people see as progress." Brighton continued to look around. "I can almost see it. We'd paint and spruce up the existing barn. That would be for the goats and sheep, because we would need to enlarge the flocks a little. We'd build another barn a little ways away for the ponies, cows, and a few pigs. Add a rabbit hutch, where we could let the kids pet them. They couldn't pet all the animals, of course, but they could see them and get close to them." The energy in Brighton's voice was catching. "What do you think?"

"Me?" Tanner asked. He wasn't sure he was qualified to have an opinion. He understood animals and things like that. He wasn't a business kind of guy.

"Sure, you. I really want you to be part of this."

"Why?" Tanner asked. "I'm j… j… just the guy you hired."

Brighton stared at him openmouthed and then moved closer. "I don't think you are."

Tanner didn't understand what Brighton meant. He was the guy Brighton had hired to help around the farm. There was no denying that. Whatever feelings Tanner might have thought he had or whatever he might have imagined could have been going on between them, he'd given it a lot of thought over the past couple of days, and he knew he couldn't go through what he'd been through with Royce again. He couldn't chance it. All of that had taken the wind out of his sails, and it had taken months for him to feel like himself again. "Yes, I am," Tanner corrected.

Brighton deflated like a balloon with a hole in it. "Do you really think that?" He took a step closer. "After that kiss, do you really think that? I don't go around kissing every guy who comes along. I never have. And I don't jump into bed with every guy I meet either."

Tanner winced and turned away. That really hurt, and Tanner didn't know why. Brighton certainly hadn't said it on purpose. He couldn't know what had happened.

"Tanner," Brighton said gently, and he turned back around. Brighton held out his hand. "I can't do this alone."

84

"Is that why you're doing this… with me?" Tanner left his hand by his side. Brighton didn't answer his question. Rather he held his hand steady and cocked his eyebrow slightly. Tanner knew Brighton wasn't the kind to get close to someone to get what he wanted, and he slowly extended his arm, taking Brighton's hand.

It was warm and felt comforting in his. Brighton curled his fingers around his and tugged him closer. It wasn't forceful, just enough to let Tanner know what Brighton wanted. He moved closer to Brighton and was about to take him in his arms when a car turned into the drive. Tanner pulled away, and their hands separated. He turned as the car pulled to a stop, turned around, and went back the way it came.

"Come inside," Brighton whispered. "You need to get cleaned up."

"I still have work to do," Tanner whispered. "The yard needs cutting, and I still need to fix that fence rail at the sheep pen."

Brighton nodded. "I have work I need to do as well." He took a step back, but the heat in Brighton's eyes made Tanner pause. Then he turned and hurried out to the small shed to get the lawn mower. He needed to get busy or he wouldn't get anything done at all.

TANNER STAYED busy for the rest of the day. He went in to eat and did so quickly before going right back outside. Right after lunch a van pulled up to the house from an electrical company. The power went off everywhere, and Tanner was grateful he had plenty to keep him busy that didn't require power tools. In the midafternoon, a bank of clouds rolled in and covered the sun for a while, which brought the temperature down and made it easier to work. By quitting time he'd gotten all the chores done. The barn was in better shape than it had been in years, the lawn had been mowed, and all the paddock fences had been repaired and checked one more time to ensure there would be no repeat of the sheep getting loose.

He walked to the house to tell Brighton good night. He'd already determined that he needed to put some distance between them. He'd spent all afternoon thinking, and as much as Brighton fascinated him, Tanner didn't think getting involved with him was a good idea. Yeah, he'd been the one to start it with the kissing, and if Brighton thought he was a tease, he could live with that, but it was best that he not get involved with his boss. Nothing good could come of that. The electricians looked like they were packing up. Lights were on in the house, and a soft hum emanated from up above. Brighton stepped out on the porch and watched as the men put the last of their equipment in the back of their van. Then they got in and a few minutes later pulled down the drive.

"I have air-conditioning now," Brighton said. "At least in my bedroom so I can sleep. The electricians installed a window unit." He stepped carefully to the edge of the porch. "Did you mull through what's been bothering you?" Tanner stepped back in surprise. "I'm not oblivious, Tanner. I saw the way you wouldn't look at me at lunch, and then all afternoon you've been working like a man possessed, like someone trying to either figure something out or work hard enough to forget something. Maybe both. So did you make your decision?"

"I guess," Tanner answered.

Brighton moved back and sat in his chair. "I see." He held his cane, not taking his eyes off Tanner. "I guess I should have expected that answer." He shifted his gaze down to his legs. "It was foolish of me to think you might be interested in someone who can barely walk." Tanner could hardly hear him; Brighton spoke so softly.

"You think…," Tanner began, but the words threatened to come tumbling out, and he knew it would be a mess of sounds that would make no sense, so he put a stop to it so he wouldn't sound like a fool. "You think that I…. I don't see you like that!" Tanner said the words with more force than he intended, but not more than he felt.

"Then why?" Brighton asked. "I could understand if it was about my leg. Who wants to get involved with a guy who's twenty-eight years old and walks like an old man?"

Tanner felt his resolve slipping away. "It's not your leg. It's me."

Brighton rolled his eyes. "That's the oldest line in the book." He stood up and took a few slow steps toward the door. "It's okay, Tanner. I understand."

Tanner watched as Brighton pulled open the door and stepped inside. This was one of those moments—he knew it. Like in the movies, when the hero needs to make a decision, and he usually makes the wrong one and spends the rest of the movie wishing he'd done something different. Tanner didn't want that, so he took a step forward and caught the screen door before it snapped closed. He held it and stepped inside. Brighton turned around, watching him.

Tanner let the screen door close behind him and then pushed the front door closed.

"What do you want, Tanner?" Brighton asked in a whisper.

"It has nothing to do with your legs," Tanner said. "I d… don't see your legs or the c… cane. Just you."

"That's nice, Tanner. Not many people do that."

"I know you hear me and not the st… stutter." Tanner moved closer. He had to make sure Brighton wanted this as much as he did. Tanner could admit he wanted Brighton. That was the easy part. He had no doubt about that. What scared him was what came after. That was when things fell apart before.

Brighton took a step toward him, and Tanner threw caution to the wind. He took Brighton in his arms and held him close. Brighton's cane thumped on the floor, and then Tanner was being held in return.

Tanner brought his lips to Brighton's, tasting him, reveling in his earthy sweetness and warmth. He loved the way Brighton's lips felt against his, firm and yet soft. Tanner cupped the back of Brighton's head, deepening the kiss. He felt Brighton press against him and without thinking held him tight. Brighton's legs had this habit of going out from under him, and Tanner wasn't going to let that happen. He swept Brighton off his feet and into his arms.

"What are you doing?" Brighton asked, half chuckling.

"What I wanted to d… do last time." Tanner moved toward the stairs and began to climb. He held Brighton to him, maintaining balance. When he reached the top, he followed Brighton's gaze to his bedroom. He opened the door and carried Brighton inside, then laid him down on the bed.

He was a sweaty, dirty mess. His shirt was streaked with dust and bits of grass. "I need to use your shower if I c… can. I d… don't want to make a mess of… everything."

"It's down the hall," Brighton said tentatively.

"I won't be long. I promise." Tanner left the room and hurried down the hall. Then he stopped and bounded down the stairs. He scooped Brighton's cane off the floor and ran it back upstairs. He opened the bedroom door, set the cane just inside, and hurried to the bathroom.

Tanner started the water and stripped off his clothes. Then he stepped into the shower. He didn't care if the water was cold. All he wanted was to get the dirt and stink off him. He grabbed the soap from the dish, lathered his hands, and scrubbed himself clean in world-record time. He found some shampoo and scrubbed his hair before rinsing all the soap off. He stepped out of the shower, grabbed a towel, and dried himself.

Sweat began to form almost as soon as he wrapped the towel around his waist and stepped out of the bathroom. He left the door open to give the excess moisture somewhere to go and then pushed open the door to Brighton's bedroom. He stepped inside. Brighton lay on the bed, shoes off but otherwise still dressed. He turned toward him and stopped still.

"My God, you're amazing," Brighton whispered. He shifted to move closer. "I wasn't sure what you wanted me to do so I waited for you." He began to blush deeply. "You're almost naked." He smiled and sat up on the edge of the bed. Tanner moved closer and tugged at the tail of Brighton's shirt.

He was wearing way too much. Tanner pulled off the shirt, then tossed it on the floor out of the way. Then he leaned forward, kissing Brighton back as he pushed him back onto the bed. The cool room chilled Tanner's skin, but Brighton's hands instantly warmed him.

Brighton broke the kiss, panting a little. "What do you see in me?" he asked, blushing once again.

"Y... you're b... b... beautiful." Tanner had never mastered the art of soft talk. Whenever he tried, he always stuttered terribly, so he decided to keep quiet. He placed his hands on Brighton, stroking his silky chest and belly. He stopped at his belt, trying to decide what he wanted to do. Brighton held his breath and sucked in his belly, thrusting his hips forward in a sign of exactly what he wanted. Tanner unfastened Brighton's belt and tugged open his pants before pulling them down his legs and dropping them on the floor with Brighton's shirt.

Brighton's briefs were tented. Brighton blushed again, as though his arousal was something to be ashamed of. From what Tanner could see, it was more like something to be proud of. He gently parted Brighton's legs and stepped between them. Tanner carefully leaned over Brighton, capturing his lips in a deep kiss that curled his own toes. Brighton gripped his back, caressing his skin. When Brighton reached his waist, he tugged at the towel, and it came loose. Tanner lifted his hips, and Brighton pulled the towel away. It most likely ended up on the floor with everything else; Tanner didn't take the time to look. He pressed his chest to Brighton's, skin to skin, and the sensation took his breath away. Tanner wound his arms under Brighton and then rolled them on the bed so Brighton's weight now pressed against him.

That was hot. "Tanner... I." Brighton paused and lifted his lips away.

Tanner cradled Brighton's cheeks in his big hands, hoping Brighton would tell him why he'd stopped. "I don't want to hurt you," he said measuredly in order to keep from stuttering. "I like how you feel." He brought Brighton's lips to his, kissing him, holding Brighton as close as he possibly could. He slid his hands down Brighton's back, caught the waistband of his briefs, and pushed them down. He wanted nothing between them at all, and soon he'd accomplished that. He shifted them on the bed until Brighton's head rested on the pillow. He made sure he was nice and comfortable before licking his way down Brighton's neck.

Brighton shivered under him, moaning softly. Tanner loved that sound. It told him more than paragraphs of spoken words. He continued his explorations, listening for more moans and to the way Brighton's breathing changed. Panting told Tanner he'd found one of those special spots, like just above his hip, and when he nipped lightly at one of Brighton's small pink nipples, or when he swirled his tongue in Brighton's belly button.

Tanner knelt between Brighton's spread legs, pausing just to look up at him. Brighton's eyes were closed, and he breathed shallowly, excitement crackling the air.

"Tanner, please...." Brighton whimpered. "No one has touched me since...." Brighton stopped, and Tanner stared at him.

"S... since the accident?" Tanner asked.

"Yeah," Brighton admitted. Tanner shifted slightly. Brighton's right leg from knee to hip was a network of scars, some jagged and some neat, most likely from surgery. Tanner wanted to ask about everything that had happened, but now wasn't the time. He settled back on his haunches and trailed his hand over Brighton's scarred leg, touching lightly but spreading his warmth along Brighton's leg.

The muscles were as tight as a lame horse's. Tanner slowly rubbed up and down. He looked at the bedside table and grabbed a small tube of lotion. He spread some on his hand and began to rub, working it into the skin, making it soft and allowing his hands to easily glide without too much friction. "Feel good?"

Brighton whimpered softly. "Yes."

"Tell me if it hurts," Tanner said.

"It doesn't." Brighton closed his eyes and seemed to soak in the attention. "I had a boyfriend before the accident." Brighton flinched and then relaxed once again. Tanner noted to be extra careful with the outside of Brighton's knee. "He left me while I was still in the hospital. He couldn't take the fact that I might not be able to walk again. He didn't even stick around long enough to find out what would happen. He just left."

This was not how he'd imagined this going. Tanner had expected him and Brighton to go at it hot and heavy. Instead, the evening had veered off in a direction he had never seen it going. "He was a b… bastard!" Tanner continued stroking lightly, his movements getting longer until he stroked from hip to knee. It was important to him that Brighton know that his leg didn't bother him. It was just part of who Brighton was. He continued stroking, and soon Brighton moaned softly once again.

Tanner shifted and stroked up and down Brighton's chest and belly. They could talk about their pasts later—not that he wanted to do that at all, but at least it could wait. He put all that out of his mind, leaned over Brighton, and kissed him hard.

Brighton slid his arms around Tanner's neck, holding him tight, communicating clearly that he wasn't going to let go anytime soon. Tanner didn't want to put too much weight on Brighton, but Brighton pulled him down and held tight.

The excitement that had waned while he was massaging Brighton's leg returned with a vengeance. Tanner once again rolled them on the bed and held Brighton close. He loved the feel of him in his arms and never wanted it to end. Brighton pushed away, pressing on Tanner's shoulders. "Just stay right there, big guy." He grinned and slid downward.

Brighton stroked his shoulders and then over his chest. Tanner closed his eyes and reveled in the sensation of being touched like this. Brighton tweaked his nipples. Tanner gasped when Brighton licked and sucked at them, scraping his teeth just enough to send a ripple of fire through him. Damn, he loved that, and he pressed his chest forward. Brighton sucked harder, tweaking the other nipple between his fingers. "Brighton…."

"You like that, don't you?" Brighton asked, lifting his head slightly so their gazes met. Tanner nodded. Brighton smiled wickedly and slid further down Tanner's body. He stroked Tanner's chest while licking down his belly.

Tanner held his breath, hoping Brighton would go further. He did. Tanner whimpered like a baby when Brighton took the head of his cock between his sweet lips. When he sucked harder, taking more of him into his hot mouth, Tanner swallowed and tried to think whether anything had ever felt so good in his life. Nothing came to mind. There was nothing close. His past didn't compare, and when Brighton sucked him completely to the root, he thrust his hips forward, lifting Brighton right off the bed. And Brighton stayed right with him. "Jesus...," he groaned.

Brighton didn't answer. Instead, he hummed softly, sending vibrations of delight up Tanner's cock and through his entire body. Brighton bobbed his head, and Tanner gripped the sheets in his fists, hoping like hell he didn't tear them as he damn near forgot his name. Thankfully, Brighton slowed down; otherwise, Tanner wouldn't last much longer, and it was way too early for things to be over. He wanted it to last and last.

Tanner guided Brighton back down onto the bed. He sucked at Brighton's nipples and tasted along his belly, laving the warm skin.

"It's been a long time, Tanner...."

He smiled and sucked Brighton's thick cock between his lips, the head sliding over his tongue. Tanner sighed. He loved that feeling, though Brighton was thicker than any he'd had before, and well... he was perfect. He'd had some books he'd kept under his bed at the ranch so no one would ever see. Naughty stories, but he tried some of the things they had in them, and damn if Brighton didn't whimper when he ran his tongue just below the underside of the head. And though he thought Brighton's skin tasted good, this was like Brighton amplified, and he sucked harder, bobbing his head.

Brighton placed a hand on his head and gently stopped him. "I'm not gonna last, and...."

Tanner stopped. "What do you w... want to do?" He felt so awkward. Brighton rolled to the side and pulled open the drawer of the bedside table. He brought out a small bottle and placed it on the stand. Then he handed a condom to Tanner. He had his answer as clear as if Brighton had described it in detail.

Brighton started to roll over, and Tanner got out of the way. Brighton rested on his belly, his butt in the air. "I know this isn't the most romantic position, but it's how it's most comfortable. I think."

Tanner set the condom aside and straddled Brighton's legs, careful to keep his weight off them. Then he scooted upward until his cock rested in the cleft between Brighton's cheeks. He leaned forward and stroked up and down Brighton's back, sliding his dick along Brighton's skin. "Are you sure?" he asked into Brighton's ear.

"Oh yes," Brighton answered with a little shiver that coursed through him and right into Tanner. That excitement was catching, and he thrust his hips slightly. "It's been a while, so go slow."

Tanner licked along Brighton's shoulder blade, and when Brighton turned his way, he kissed him. It was sloppy and awkward, but at least he didn't feel completely cut off from him.

"Yeah," Brighton whimpered and thrust back against him. Tanner slid down Brighton's back. He rested on the bed next to him, stroking his butt and then between his legs, cupping Brighton's balls and then sliding along Brighton's cock before retreating to stroke his butt again. Tanner kept contact with Brighton as he reached for the bottle to slick his fingers.

He slid a finger between Brighton's cheeks to his opening, teasing the skin before pressing for entry. Brighton groaned and thrust back against him. Tanner loved the tight heat around him and took his cues from Brighton. Once he was begging and telling him he was ready, Tanner rolled on the condom and got into position. "Brighton," Tanner whispered and pressed his cock to Brighton's entrance. The last thing he wanted to do was hurt him. He was quickly coming to the realization that maybe they had both been hurt. Lord knew he had. Tanner wasn't going to hurt anyone if he could help it, and the thought of causing Brighton pain made him stop right at the gate.

"Tanner," Brighton moaned and pressed back against him. Tanner pressed forward, and Brighton's body opened to him, gripping him as he moved inside. The heat short-circuited his brain, and the pressure… God, he could barely stop himself from coming right there. He thought unsexy thoughts for a few seconds as he sank further and further into Brighton's exquisite body.

Every instinct pushed him to go faster, but he stopped, remembering he wouldn't let himself hurt Brighton. Tanner halted, his cock throbbing and jumping while he waited for Brighton to adjust. Then he sank the rest of the way, releasing the breath he'd been holding.

"Please," Brighton whispered. Tanner held still once again and then, slowly, began to withdraw.

"Won't hurt you," Tanner whispered, and he lightly sucked on Brighton's ear. Damn, the man tasted good, and he continued sucking and then moved to his shoulder, licking the tender skin as Brighton quivered under him.

"Not hurting." Brighton pushed back against him, and Tanner withdrew. Then he held still, and Brighton pressed backward. Tanner didn't move, letting Brighton set the pace. He raised and lowered his hips, fucking himself on Tanner's cock. He'd always been the one in control, but damn if Brighton wasn't a firecracker willing to take what he wanted. Tanner held his hips still and wrapped an arm under Brighton, holding him around the chest.

"T… take what you want."

Brighton seemed intent on doing just that. He moved faster and faster, tightening up his lithe body, and it drove Tanner out of his mind. He had no idea giving up a little control to someone else could feel so amazing. He'd tried it once before, and it hadn't worked out so well. But this… God.

"Tanner!" Brighton cried. Tanner held him tight, pressed him to the mattress, and took control. He snapped his hips. Not hard enough to hurt, but from the small yelps that morphed into moans, he had it just right.

Tanner's breathing quickened, and he drove faster. Brighton met each thrust, filling the room with groans and cries that got louder and louder and drove Tanner's desire higher and higher. He never wanted this to stop, but his legs were already tingling, and he felt the start of his climax building at the base of his spine. His thrusting became erratic, but he was determined to wait for Brighton.

"Tanner, I'm—" Brighton cried throatily. Tanner kept up the rhythm as steadily as he could. Brighton clenched and relaxed around him. "God!" Brighton tightened around him holding his cock in a vise grip as he moaned loudly and shook through his release. Tanner followed right behind, the throes of Brighton's passion pulling him over the edge. Tanner clamped his eyes closed as wave after wave of pure pleasure washed over him. He held still and did his best not to collapse on top of Brighton.

Tanner ended up on the bed next to him, wincing when their bodies disconnected. He had no choice; he gasped for breath, and his arms felt like jelly. When he came back to himself, Tanner pulled off the condom, tied it off, and placed it in the trash before gently curling his arms around Brighton's chest, pulling them together.

Neither of them spoke for quite a while. Tanner gently rubbed Brighton's smooth skin, keeping his eyes closed so he could impress every sensation onto his memory. "This is nice," Brighton sighed, shifting closer. "It's been a while since I was with someone... like that."

"Yeah?" Tanner asked. He already knew some of the answer, but he didn't want Brighton to stop. If he was willing to talk, then Tanner was willing to listen.

"His name is Kurt, and we went out for almost a year. I was driving home from his apartment. I was rounding the traffic circle a mile or so from here, and this guy came down from the freeway. He didn't stop like he was supposed to and rammed into the passenger side of the car. Thank goodness it wasn't the driver's side, or I wouldn't have made it. As it was, the car cut my leg really bad. The worst part was the muscle and tendon damage." Brighton paused, and Tanner held him a little tighter. "I woke up in the hospital with Brianne leaning over my bed, tears running down her cheeks. She said they had to cut me out of the car and weren't sure I would live at first because I'd lost so much blood. Then they weren't sure I'd be able to keep my leg." Brighton sighed. "Sometimes I wish they had taken it. At least I wouldn't be in all this pain. The doctors say it will take time and that I should get stronger, and the pain should lessen, but it hasn't happened yet."

"Kurt left?" Tanner prompted.

"Yeah. I was in the hospital. I'd apparently been unconscious for almost a day, and then he showed up a few hours after I woke up. At first he was sympathetic and nice. Then, when he was getting ready to leave, he turned tearfully and said he couldn't do this." Brighton began breathing more heavily. Tanner didn't know what to do, so he just continued holding him. "Brianne heard him, and she told him to get his useless ass out of the room and my life. He left, but she followed him. The next thing I heard was Kurt yelping and begging her to stop kicking him. Apparently Brianne didn't, because a nurse brought her back, scolding her that no matter how big an asshole he was, hospital regulations prevented her from kicking him repeatedly."

Tanner couldn't help laughing. "D… did she really do that?"

"She did." Brighton's voice lightened, and Tanner kissed his shoulder. "We're all we have. And she can be a lioness at times. Anyway, that was the last I saw of Kurt." Brighton sighed. "We had talked about moving in together, but thankfully we hadn't gotten beyond the talking stage. What a mess that would have been."

"He didn't really love you. If he had, he wouldn't have left." Tanner closed his eyes, making small circles on Brighton's belly with his fingers.

"I know that now. But at the time it really hurt. I wasn't sure I would ever be whole again, and the person I thought loved me took one look at me in the hospital bed and walked out." Brighton's voice broke. "After that I wasn't sure I wanted to live. I was in constant pain and ended up going through multiple surgeries to put my leg back together." He sniffled a few times and blew out a deep breath. "I know I need to be patient, and it's a miracle I can walk at all, but I'd like to be strong enough not to need the cane." Brighton shifted, and Tanner moved back slightly. Brighton rolled over and faced him, placing a hand on Tanner's chest.

"It will… happen in time."

"I'm starting to wonder. But I can make it up and down the stairs easier than I used to. It's just that sometimes my knee gives out for no real reason. I'd hoped that would end, but it still happens sometimes."

"Have you tried therapy?" Tanner inquired.

"I have, and I need to go to the doctor so he can check my progress. I know he'll want me to have more therapy. I just don't want to go in case he says things are worse." Brighton closed his eyes.

Tanner tugged him closer. He chose to say nothing. He could have said it was better to know, but that was something Brighton would have to decide for himself. He'd already been through a lot, so Tanner figured he knew what was best. He turned toward the clock at the side of the bed. He opened his mouth and hesitated before saying, "Have you eaten?"

"No." Brighton sat up on the edge of the bed. "I should make us something to eat." He turned, and Tanner could almost see the question in his eyes.

"I'll help you," Tanner said as he too sat up, sliding his legs to either side of Brighton, pressing his chest to Brighton's back. "There's no hurry. We have all night." He kissed Brighton's shoulder once again. He loved holding Brighton. He felt perfect in his arms.

Brighton slowly got to his feet, and Tanner scooted over and grabbed his cane. Brighton dressed quickly and left the room. Tanner did the same, grabbing his shoes on the way out of the bedroom. He stayed out of the way as Brighton went down the stairs and met him in the kitchen.

"I'll put something together for us to eat," Brighton said.

Tanner looked out the window. "I'll check the barn." He left the house and hurried across the yard. While out there he placed his motorcycle in the garage. Then he made sure all the critters had food and water. "You did good today," Tanner said to the goats, who looked up at him and then hurried around the pen. "The boys liked you." He checked on the sheep, who were now munching away. They all lay close together like they were cold. Tanner knew it would take a little time for them to get used to their lack of covering. He collected all the wool and put it in the barn, where it would stay dry. He wondered what Brighton planned to do with it.

Tanner smiled when he thought about Brighton back in the house, making dinner for them. He knew it was way too early to be thinking about getting domestic and stuff. He sighed and pushed those thoughts out of his head. He always jumped ahead, but he needed to stop doing that. Nothing had come of it before but heartache, pain, and finding himself on the outside looking in. Granted, that wasn't an unusual feeling. He'd always felt like an outsider, thanks to his speech problem.

The pony bobbed his head, neighing softly, pulling Tanner out of his wandering thoughts. He needed to take things as they came. That was the only way. He placed some hay in Napoleon's manger and lightly patted his neck. Things were good right now, and he was happy. Tanner had to accept that and enjoy it for as long as it would last, because he knew it would end—some way, somehow it would. For him, it always did.

He closed the barn doors and walked back across the yard. He noticed that the mail was in the box, so he grabbed it and brought it inside. He placed it on the table where Brighton seemed to put it and then went through to the kitchen. The scent of bacon filled the room. Tanner's stomach rumbled as Brighton put together the last BLT sandwich at the counter.

"Cooking for an army?" Tanner asked.

Brighton turned toward him. "In case you haven't noticed, you are an army." Brighton smiled at him. "A one-man army."

"I know I'm big," Tanner began.

Brighton picked up his cane from where he'd leaned it against the cabinet. "I like you that way." He came closer. "I think it makes you sexy."

Tanner enfolded Brighton into his arms. "Royce always said he was afraid I'd crush him or something…," he confessed.

"Who's Royce?" Brighton asked. "Is he the reason you ended up here?"

Tanner nodded.

"But you aren't ready to talk about it."

Tanner shook his head. That was the last thing he wanted to discuss now. Things were going well, and that was sure to bring an end to everything.

CHAPTER 5

BRIGHTON WAS happy. The past few days had been spectacular. He'd spent a lot of his extra time working on a business plan for the farm. If he was going to make this a success, Brighton knew he would have to have detailed plans for what he wanted to put where, the animals they would need, their care, and the buildings that would have to be constructed. He also had to get cost estimates so he could figure out if he had enough money. He sincerely doubted he could do everything he wanted all at once, so he prioritized what seemed most important and what he thought could bring in money from the start.

Tanner was a huge help. While his experience was largely in ranching rather than farming, he had enough practical experience that Brighton hoped he could avoid any pitfalls.

"Wh… when do you hope to open?" Tanner asked as they sat around Brighton's kitchen table, looking at the plans he'd put together.

"Probably next spring." Brighton had hoped to open in the fall, but it wasn't going to happen. As he'd drawn up plans, he'd decided that paths had to be put in, along with a picnic area. He wanted the petting farm to be fully accessible for all children. "It's going to take time to get permits, build the buildings, and then get the animals settled. It's also too late in the year to plant the pumpkin patch, but hopefully we can get the areas plowed and prepared this fall so that we can be ready for next year." He returned to the plan.

Tanner looked it over and pointed to a few things.

Brighton nodded and said, "I figured we could put all the animals in the same area. The existing barn can be reconfigured for the sheep and goats. We'd build a new building for the other livestock and paint it red with white trim, so it looks very kid friendly. The pony ride would go near the new barn, and I thought we could add a rabbit hutch here." Brighton pointed to an area between the barns. "These will be the bathrooms over here. We can plant this section of the land as the new orchard and use part of the old area for a haunted orchard in the fall. That will also obscure the view of the strip mall. The pumpkin patch would go here, with the corn maze behind it. That would put the maze between us and the condos." Brighton smiled. "My next step is to get cost estimates for all the buildings and the livestock as well as try to estimate ongoing operational costs." It was a daunting task.

"Are you sure you want to do this?" Tanner asked. "It seems like a lot of work."

Brighton had thought about that more than once. "I really do. This is the most excited I think I've been about something since my accident." He sighed and sat back in his chair. "I think I've just been existing for the past year. I have my work, but other than that I've been going through the motions." He reached out and took Tanner's hand. "You helped me see that."

Tanner's eyes widened. "How?"

Brighton swallowed. "You wanted to be with me." He stood slowly and used the counter to steady himself. "After Kurt left, I thought no one would want to be with me." He couldn't look at Tanner right now. "The man I thought I loved and who had said he loved me walked out as soon as he was told I might not walk again." Brighton took a deep breath. "I figured that part of my life was over."

"It's not."

"I know that. Because of you." Brighton turned around. "I'm not proposing marriage or getting all heavy right now. That isn't what I'm trying to say. It's just that you've given me a gift and I don't think you know it." He walked back to the table. Tanner shot up and took Brighton's arm, helping him back to the chair.

Brighton noticed that Tanner didn't say much after all that. He had hoped that Tanner would start to open up a little, but he seemed perfectly content to keep quiet about his past. That bothered Brighton a little, and he wondered what could be so bad that Tanner wouldn't tell him about it.

"I didn't know," Tanner finally said. "And I'm glad." Tanner didn't let go of his hand, lightly stroking Brighton's fingers.

Brighton finally figured he just needed to ask. "Tanner, what happened to you?"

Tanner turned away, and his fingers stopped moving. "I.... It's...." He began stuttering intensely, and it was painful to watch. Tanner opened his mouth, but all that came out were bits of sound that made very little sense. Brighton knew he'd made a mistake.

"It's all right. I shouldn't have asked. You'll tell me when you're ready." Fuck, he saw a huge man who was strong enough to carry him upstairs as though he weighed next to nothing. But on the inside, he was hurting, and that made Brighton angry. "I'm sorry." Whoever had hurt Tanner deserved to be horsewhipped.

But the nagging in the back of his mind wouldn't go away. What could Tanner be so ashamed of? Being hurt was something that happened to a lot of people. It had happened to him, and he'd told Tanner about it. He had hoped that Tanner would open up. He hoped the hurt was maybe just too new and that Tanner needed some time. Hell, if that was all it was, then... he could be patient. But in the back of his mind he kept wondering if it was more than that. What if Tanner had done something he was truly ashamed of? What if he'd hurt someone? As soon as that thought crossed Brighton's mind, he dismissed it. Tanner was gentle and kind. He knew that. He took a deep breath and tried to silence the doubts that ran though his mind.

TWO DAYS later Brighton woke up next to Tanner, sore in all the right places. The air conditioner in the room hummed softly, and

Brighton snuggled closer to Tanner in the slightly chilly air. It was perfect.

"I gotta get up," Tanner whispered. "Feed the critters." When Tanner was relaxed like he was right now, his stutter was much less pronounced and sometimes absent, which Brighton took as a good sign.

He lightly stroked Tanner's shoulder, and he turned. Brighton smiled and shifted closer, tugging Tanner into a kiss. God, he loved Tanner's weight on him. He shifted to get comfortable as Tanner's lips covered his in a deep kiss, just short of bruising and so intense Brighton's toes curled. Tanner wound his arms around him, pressing their bodies together. His thick cock slid along Brighton's, sending ripples of heat through him. "I can barely think when I'm with you," Brighton whispered when Tanner broke their kiss, and Tanner's response was to kiss him again, deeper, and to hold him tighter.

"Mine," Tanner whispered, and that was all Brighton needed to hear. He was Tanner's, and he held him in return.

Brighton closed his eyes. He wanted Tanner inside him, but he didn't want to break contact either, so he moved with him, Brighton's cock sliding along Tanner's hip, all friction and heat as Tanner breathed softly into his ear. He wasn't sure what Tanner was saying, but it didn't matter. He was being held tight, and that was what counted.

Tanner stilled. Brighton opened his eyes, wondering what had happened and what he'd done wrong. The strong arms that held him slipped away. Brighton raised his head as Tanner pushed himself off the bed. Their gazes locked, and then Tanner's shifted, raking over him. Brighton's cock throbbed at the intensity. Tanner leaned forward and took him into his mouth.

Brighton gasped and quivered with excitement he couldn't control. Tanner took him deeper, sucking his cock to the root while he stroked up Brighton's belly to rest his hands over his chest, tweaking his nipples and stroking his skin until Brighton thought his head would explode. No one had ever made him feel like this—so alive. Every touch tingled and sent jolts of electricity from his body straight to the center of pleasure. His head throbbed and ached in the best way possible; his skin craved more, and Tanner gave it. He wanted, needed, craved... and got it all. "Tanner!" Brighton shouted when he could contain the desire no longer. His release shot from him, the last of his control bursting like a popped balloon. Tanner took it all as Brighton heaved for breath, trying to catch something that seemed as elusive as a cool breeze in the heat of summer.

Tanner let him slip from between his lips. Brighton lay back on the bed, spent and happy. He drew Tanner to him, tasting his own saltiness on Tanner's lips. That was so damn hot.

"Straddle me," Brighton whispered. Tanner didn't seem to know what he meant, so Brighton guided him until Tanner's legs were on either side of his chest. He slid between Tanner's legs, wrapped his fingers around Tanner's throbbing cock, and sucked the head between his lips. Tanner hissed and groaned as Brighton sucked and stroked him. He took him deeper and then stilled, holding Tanner in his mouth as his cock throbbed and jumped along his tongue.

And the *view*. Brighton felt his cock rising from its brief rest from that alone. Tanner's stomach rippled as he moved, chest thrust forward—a mountain of muscle and power that Brighton controlled with his lips and tongue. He sucked him deep, gaze focused upward so he didn't miss the way Tanner's cut stomach quivered and shook or the way he gasped for breath and then held it, his chest pumping outward even more. The sight alone made Brighton hard, but the feel of Tanner's cock over his tongue and the musky, rich taste drove him to utter distraction.

Brighton pulled back, leaving just the large head between his lips. He swirled his tongue around it.

Tanner gasped. "Fuck, Brighton," he whimpered and moved his hips to thrust deeper.

Brighton sucked harder, pulling Tanner deep. He held still, nose buried in Tanner's blond nest, inhaling the unique scent of him. This was amazing. Tanner smelled, tasted, and felt like heaven—his version of heaven, at least—and he wanted this to go on forever. Hell, he needed it to. Brighton felt alive; he *was* alive, in a way he had never been before. Heart, soul, body, spirit—they were all engaged and running at full steam. This had to be that special engagement that he'd heard could be so magical. He'd never had it with Kurt, not in the entire time they were together, but with Tanner…. His excitement took over. Brighton bobbed his head, sucking hard, then pulled off. "Is this what you want?" Brighton asked. "Tell me."

"Yes," Tanner cried, locking his hands behind his head, stretching. "Suck me! Please."

Brighton did, industrial strength this time.

"Fuck yeah!" Tanner rocked his hips.

Brighton sucked him hard and deep, losing himself in the pleasure he was giving. He began stroking himself. It didn't matter that he'd just come; he was so fucking turned on by Tanner he couldn't control himself.

"Jesus," Tanner cried when Brighton sucked him all the way in and held still. Tanner throbbed, and Brighton held him, releasing his own cock and clamping his hands on to Tanner's hard ass. Then he backed away and sucked him deep again and again, pushing Tanner's ass to meet him.

Tanner went wild, writhing above him. "Not gonna last!"

Brighton didn't want to stop to tell him he didn't want him to, so he sucked harder, pulling Tanner's release from him. Tanner bucked and then held still. Brighton sucked him and felt Tanner throb. His mouth filled with Tanner's release, and he swallowed hard, again and again, taking everything Tanner had to offer. He wanted it all, and he made sure he got it.

Tanner didn't move for a long time. Brighton rested his head back on the pillow, Tanner's cock dripping onto his chest. Brighton watched every move Tanner made as he stroked himself. Tanner reached around and batted Brighton's hand away, stroking him with a slight circular motion that stimulated that place just below the head with each and every stroke.

"Damn!" Brighton shouted, and Tanner thrust his chest forward, clenching his abs. The sight was perfect, intense, and so fucking hot that Brighton lost control for a second time. Heat splashed on his belly, and his mind floated on the intensity of two climaxes in less than half an hour. He gasped and flopped back on the bed like a wrung-out rag doll. He had nothing more.

Tanner unstraddled him and lay on the bed, stroking up his belly and chest, rubbing Brighton's release into his skin. Tanner leaned over him, and Brighton felt his warm breath on his lips. He opened his mouth, and Tanner kissed him, swirling his tongue between Brighton's lips, making a soft "mmm" sound as they savored the taste of what they'd just shared.

They lay together for a while. Brighton relaxed, half-asleep and happy as he could ever remember. He never wanted this to end. But there were things that had to be done.

Tanner sighed and tugged him closer. "I do have to get up."

The words sounded as sleepy as Brighton felt. He hummed slightly and held Tanner a little tighter. He wanted just a few more minutes.

"I'll make some breakfast." Brighton wanted to roll over and go back to sleep, but if Tanner was getting up to take care of his animals, then he figured he should get out of bed as well. He had things he needed to do, but none of them were as pleasant sounding as spending the day in bed.

Tanner got dressed, and Brighton watched. He loved his cowboy's tan legs and white ass, but hated that they were disappearing into a pair of jeans. He gasped slightly when Tanner buttoned his fly and turned to him with a wicked wink. Brighton was going to be thinking naughty thoughts all day knowing Tanner wasn't wearing anything under those jeans that framed his butt like a fine work of art. Hell, Tanner's ass was a work of art, a miracle of nature that, given the chance, Brighton intended to celebrate as much as possible.

Brighton got to his feet after cleaning up, carefully began dressing as well. He had work that had to get done today, so he planned to eat and then sit at his desk for as long as he could manage. Tanner left after giving him a kiss, and Brighton finished getting dressed, then headed to the kitchen. He prepared breakfast and set the fixings aside until Tanner came back in. Then he figured he should go through the mail that had been piling up. He brought it all to the kitchen table and peered outside to see if Tanner was heading in yet. He'd already started the coffee, and the scent filled the kitchen. He needed that so badly. Once it was done, he poured a mug and took it to the table as well. Then he sat down and started sorting. He put the bills in one pile and set the junk mail in another pile to throw away. The magazines, which there were plenty of, he sorted. His grandfather must have paid every subscription bill that had come to the house because there were twelve magazines that Brighton had received so far, and some of them had to have originally been his grandmother's.

He opened the last few pieces of mail to figure out what to do with them. Some he put aside to send on to the lawyer and others he put with the bills to pay for the farm. But one from the city made him curious. Brighton opened it and read through the details. "Son of a bitch!" He stared at the letter, seething.

"What's wrong?" Tanner asked as he came in from the living room. Brighton had been so engrossed in the details of the letter that he hadn't even heard Tanner come in.

"There's a hearing next week. The city wants to change the zoning of the land. According to this, the land hasn't been used for commercial farming for over ten years, so they want to rezone." Brighton threw the letter on the table. "I bet my relatives are behind this."

Tanner picked up the letter from the table and walked over to Brighton. After a couple of minutes, he set down the letter and pointed toward the bottom. The letter said even with the new zoning, the land could still be used for agribusiness, but would also be open for development. "I b... bet it's t... taxes."

Brighton read through the letter and nodded. "Shit. This is going to raise the value of the property through the roof, and then they'll make me pay taxes on the higher value." He could see all his plans sprouting wings and flying out the window. The additional taxes would eat up any chance he had of building the business. He'd have to sell just to meet the tax burden. "My uncle knew about this."

Tanner stared at him.

"He said something at the funeral. That it wasn't over or something like that. I bet this has been in the works, and they were waiting for Grandpa to die. They couldn't do this to him, but now that he's gone they're going to try to do it to me."

Tanner moved closer, gently pulled him to his feet, and then encased him in those strong arms of his. There was something about being held by this man—he was so strong and made Brighton feel like everything was going to be okay. That was part of what scared him: Kurt had made him feel the same way. Tanner was not Kurt, though, and he needed to remember that.

"It says there's a hearing," Tanner whispered into his ear. "They say that the l… l… land has not been actively farmed, but it has. Call Arthur and see what he says. I also suggest you f…f… finish the plans for what you want to do. Take pictures of the farm, including the f… f… fleece we harvested and the animals you have."

Brighton stopped shaking and picked up the paper from the table without moving away. "Yeah. I guess I better know what the law is so I can fight it." He took a deep breath.

"Go call, and I'll finish making breakfast."

Brighton didn't want to move away from Tanner, but he did anyway. He got his cane from where it leaned against the chair and went into the living room. He sat on the sofa, pulled up the lawyer's number from his phone, and made the call.

"I'd like to speak to Arthur, please. This is Brighton McKenzie," he said when the receptionist answered the call. She said she would connect him.

"More trouble with the relatives?" Arthur said when he came on the line. It had become a joke between them.

"I don't know. The city wants to change the zoning of the farm to allow commercial development." Brighton read him portions of the letter. "I think they want to be able to raise the taxes." He explained what he thought and what Tanner had said.

"I think Tanner's right. I'll check the codes to see what they're basing the change on, and we'll figure out how to fight this. Send me a copy of the letter, and I'll get right on it."

"I'll send it with Tanner tonight," Brighton said.

"Don't worry. There are ways we can fight this. Let me do some research," Arthur said. For a second Brighton wondered how much it was going to cost in legal fees, but then he remembered it was going to cost him a hell of a lot more in increased taxes. "Just send me the letter."

"I will," Brighton agreed. "And thank you." He hung up and returned to the kitchen. Tanner had breakfast on the table. "Your cousin said the same thing you did, that there are ways I can fight this."

Tanner nodded and sat down across from him. "Yes. L... learn the rules and use them." Tanner smiled and began to eat. Brighton did the same, but he wasn't really hungry. After a few bites of egg, he felt full, and his stomach rumbled, not in a good way. He sat back, and his stomach settled after a few seconds. He ate some more and tried to let his concerns go for now.

"Will you take the letter to Arthur this evening?" Brighton placed it on the table next to him. He hated asking that question because it meant Tanner would be leaving at the end of his workday. He loved having Tanner with him, but Tanner didn't stay every night, and his doing so would probably be rushing into things.

Tanner nodded.

It was hard for Brighton to know what Tanner was thinking most of the time. His face could be very expressive, but Brighton was learning that happened only when Tanner wanted it to. He would make a great poker player because sometimes his face revealed nothing, and he didn't talk enough to let Brighton know what was going on. It could be exasperating at times, like right now. "What do you want to say?" he prompted, because of the way Tanner kept looking at him.

"I was g… going to s… say that I had to go after work because Alicia asked me to watch the b… boys for her." Tanner's nervous stutter was back.

"Of course. Why would telling me that make you nervous?" Brighton took Tanner's hand. "Just say what you want. I'll do my best to listen."

Tanner shrugged. "I'm not used to talking much." He looked down at his plate. Brighton released his hand, and Tanner returned to his breakfast. Once he'd cleaned the plate, Tanner took his dishes to the sink. When he returned he gave Brighton a smile, squeezed his hand, and then left the house. Brighton watched as he hurried out past the animal barn to the equipment shed at the far edge of the property. Brighton hadn't been in that area yet, but he figured he needed to see what was out there. He hadn't given it much thought with the other things he had on his mind. When Tanner came back in, he'd ask him what was there.

Brighton finished eating and figured he'd try to get some work done. After taking care of the dishes, he sat at his desk and got to work. At first he had a difficult time getting started. His mind wouldn't settle on the task at hand. But after a while, the other things drifted to the back of his mind, and he immersed himself in his work.

A knock on the front door jarred him out of his thoughts. Brighton looked at the clock on his computer and realized he'd been working for two hours. He was sweating as the heat of the day had permeated the room, but he hadn't noticed. It was time for him to move anyway, so he got up and opened the front door. Aunt Vera stood on the porch, smiling at him. A crocodile in a sundress and pantyhose, he was certain.

"Good morning," he said pleasantly, wondering why she was here. He pushed open the door, and she stepped inside. "It's a little warm." Brighton made a note that he needed to get another air conditioner for the main portion of the house. At this point, central air was out of the question. The cost of installing it in the old house would be more than he could afford, especially since he wanted to keep as much money as he could for the changes to the farm.

"I see that," she said looking around. "This old house never seems to change. It's just like it was when I was little."

"Then why do you want it gone?" Brighton asked, and Aunt Vera's smile faded just a little.

"I don't. Even if you sell, the house wouldn't necessarily go. It has good bones, and it's a great place to live." She continued looking around.

There were times when Brighton didn't get her at all. Well, he was determining that he didn't understand most people as well as he thought he did. He had thought he was a people person, but that seemed to be a delusion. "Did you stop by to talk?" he prompted. "Because we can move to the porch." For some reason he wanted her out of his house.

"I suppose I—" She sighed, and Brighton realized she was stalling for some reason.

"I heard from a friend that the city was going to change the zoning." At least she had the grace not to smile. "This area is growing and will continue to grow. You can't stand in the way of progress."

"Aunt Vera, I know what you want and…."

"Brighton." She shook her head dramatically. "I know what you think, and I was wrong to be selfish. This has nothing to do with me or your uncle. This has to do with what's right for you." She swept around her. "The house needs work, and the farm is a shadow of what it once was and surrounded by condos and strip centers. Sometimes things happen for a reason." She placed her hand on his shoulder, and the gesture seemed motherly and caring. "Trying to make something out of this other than using it for the land is fruitless. Daddy knew that. He simply lived here. There used to be flocks of animals, and we used to have a lot more land. That's how Daddy survived all these years. He sold the land that's the strip mall and part of the condo complex. The farm hasn't brought in money in years."

Brighton nodded. He was sure that was true, and it made sense.

"Is being a farmer what you really want to do?" She glanced over at his computer sitting on the desk. "You have other things in your life, other interests that have nothing to do with feeding animals at five in the morning, worrying if the crops will grow, or if there will be enough or too much rain. The orchard used to bring in a lot of money, but what's left of it is really old, and the trees don't produce much anymore." Aunt Vera sighed. "None of us is getting any younger. This farm has had its time, and now it's time to move on." She stepped back and smiled. "I'm truly sorry for my bad behavior." She turned toward the door. "I have an appointment, but more than anything I wanted to see how you were doing." She smiled and pulled Brighton into a hug. It surprised him, and eventually he hugged her back. Then she turned and left the house.

Brighton walked to the front door and saw her turn and wave before getting into her Cadillac and slowly heading down the drive. He stepped away from the door, leaving it open so the breeze could blow through the house, then sat at his desk to get back to work. He hoped his aunt was being honest and telling him the truth. He wanted to believe her, and maybe she was right. The house, the farm, everything needed work—things he couldn't do. He shook his head. His aunt had been very right about one thing: he had never, ever seen himself as a farmer. He'd been a computer geek even back in school. That was where his expertise lay, not in animals and crops.

He needed to think and decide what he wanted for the long term. If he decided to go ahead with this business idea, then he had to be in it for the long haul. It wasn't like he could go into this and then just walk away in a few years. He would be developing a business, and that took time and effort. Was he willing to put in that effort? The excited energy that had sustained him for the past little while drained away, and he found himself once again right back at the beginning, wondering what he was going to do. He closed the lid on his laptop and grabbed the cord. He was hot as hell and decided to go up to his room where it was cool.

He made it up the stairs by leaving his cane behind. At the top of the stairs, he prayed his knee didn't give out and walked to his bedroom. He arrived in one piece and spent a few minutes setting up his bed as a work area before plugging in his laptop and getting comfortable. He had everything he needed and was thankful he had his phone in his pocket. He couldn't hear anything outside the room because of the air conditioner, but he was able to concentrate.

Hours passed. Brighton's hunger and the growing stiffness in his leg forced him to move from the comfort and quiet. He opened the door and listened, hearing deep, steady rumbling sounds in the distance. He made his way down the stairs and managed to get to his cane without falling on his face. The rumbling got louder, and Brighton realized it was the sound of a large engine getting closer. He pushed the curtain aside in time to see Tanner roll past the window, sitting on an old tractor. Brighton stepped outside onto the porch. "What's this?" he asked when the engine quieted.

Tanner pointed toward the shed. "I fixed it." He turned, and Brighton followed his gaze. "I plowed a portion of the field near the orchard." He smiled. "Now we look like a farm." Brighton couldn't argue with that. Hell, Tanner sitting on the tractor made them like a hunk farm. "I'll spread the muck from the barn on the field for fertilizer."

"We should spread it where we intend to plant the corn maze. Though the neighbors aren't going to like it," Brighton added with a shrug. "Let's try to do it when we know it will rain. That will help keep the smell down."

Tanner nodded and climbed down from the tractor. "Why not there by the orchard?"

"I did some research. Fruit trees require sweet soil, and manure adds acid. Maybe we can get some lime to add to the soil and decide the kind of trees to plant. It's too hot to do it now, but we can get the area ready for next spring."

"Oh." Tanner sounded disappointed.

"Thank you," Brighton said. It did make the place appear alive as opposed to sleepy like when he'd first arrived, and now everyone who drove by would be able to see that. The doubts and second-guessing from earlier seemed like something from the distant past. "You did great, and it does help the place look good." He grinned with excitement, and Tanner picked up some of the energy.

"Was someone here?" Tanner asked. "No one bothered you, did they?"

"It was my aunt." Brighton was still trying to make sense of that visit. "She behaved herself." He decided to leave it at that. He was still convinced his aunt was simply after the money, but what she'd said did make sense. So did what Tanner had done. The thing was, what his aunt had said made Brighton think and second-guess, while Tanner plowing up a small portion of the land made him elated. Maybe he was cut out to be a farmer after all. Only time would tell.

Tanner narrowed his gaze, clearly skeptical.

"She hasn't changed her spots, I know that. But she was nice. Whether that's permanently nice or just a ploy to get her way has yet to be seen." He wasn't stupid. Aunt Vera could be manipulative, and Brighton still wasn't convinced that she wasn't behind this whole zoning change. "Come in for lunch."

He held open the door, and Tanner went inside. Brighton followed him, the door banging closed. He leaned on his cane, watching Tanner move toward the kitchen. For a huge man, he was incredibly graceful, at least to him. Brighton loved the way he made the thin fabric of his T-shirt and jeans shimmer as he moved. What Tanner saw in him was a mystery, and Brighton slowly pulled into himself, arms crossing over his chest.

Tanner turned around. "Why aren't y… you coming?" He stopped and walked back to where Brighton stood. Then he grinned and lifted Brighton off his feet, hoisting him over his shoulder.

"Going caveman on me?" Brighton said with a laugh.

"Me hungry," Tanner grunted, and Brighton laughed harder.

"You can put me down." He swatted Tanner's butt, and then because of access, he grabbed his firm cheeks. "On second thought, this is a really great view."

Tanner set him down, and Brighton got the stuff out for sandwiches from the refrigerator. He'd have to call Brianne to go grocery shopping. He needed just about everything, again.

"This afternoon I need to go. Is that okay?" Tanner began making his sandwich.

"Of course."

"I'll be back in time for the evening chores," Tanner added hastily.

"It's fine. I have a lot of work I need to do. Take the truck if you want." It wasn't like he was going to need it. He made his sandwich and began eating slowly. He was happy, and when Tanner smiled across the table at him, Brighton's heart warmed. More than anything he wanted to believe that things were going to work out for him in the love department. Tanner was warm and kind. When he took Brighton's hand, his touch was gentle and caring. Sure, it was a little difficult to eat a sandwich one-handed, but he made it work.

When they were finished, Tanner cleared the table and then leaned forward and gave him a kiss. "I'll be back later."

"Okay." Brighton followed him to the front of the house. He closed the door behind him and then headed upstairs to go back to work. Before he settled in, he called Brianne and arranged for her come by that afternoon to take him to the store. Arthur called just as he hung up to tell him that they had a decent case with the zoning board, and that once he got the letter, he'd arrange for them to get together to discuss strategy. Things might just work out.

BRIGHTON WORKED hard for the next few hours. He completed a project, sent the details to the client, and received payment on his invoice, the money already deposited in his PayPal account. That would come in handy. He still had more to do but couldn't sit still any longer. He set his computer aside and sat up. He remembered he had an old backpack and had seen it at some point in the move. He hobbled to the closet and found it on the top shelf. After getting it down, he put his computer and power cord in it and slung it on his back.

Now he had both hands free to steady himself as he navigated the stairs, which he hated, but going up and down them was helping his leg, he thought. For the last few days he'd had less pain at night and—knock on wood—he hadn't fallen. Maybe like other things in his life, his leg had finally decided to cooperate.

A bank of clouds had rolled in, making the temperature bearable, so he dropped the backpack on one of the living room chairs and went to the kitchen. He got himself a glass of iced tea and made his way outside to the porch. It would be nice to sit and rock for a while.

Well, he revised that opinion as soon as he got outside, since the closeness of the air had him sweating within seconds. He sat down anyway and rocked in the chair. Despite the heat, he felt good. He sat for nearly an hour. He finished the iced tea and decided to have another. He'd gotten up to go back inside, the sun having come out again, when a strange car pulled into the driveway. The old thing looked like it had been through hell, caked with dust and dirt. As it got closer, Brighton thought that maybe it wasn't as old as he thought, just dirty. "Can I help you?" he asked as a man got out, staring over the roof of the car. He was tall and broad, with a tanned complexion, jet-black hair, and a cowboy hat with a band of silver studs.

"I sure hope so. I'm looking for Tanner Houghton. I tracked him down to his cousins, and the nice lady on the phone said he worked here." He looked around. "Doesn't look like much, but then I'm from out West, where even on a small spread the land goes from horizon to horizon."

That raised Brighton's hackles instantly. The farm might not be much, but some stranger disparaging it was almost enough for him to tell the fucker to get lost and learn some manners. "And you are?"

The man came around the car and bounded up onto the porch. "Royce Weston. I'm Tanner's boyfriend. I came to bring him back with me. There was a whole hubbub back home that I straightened out, and I came this whole way to find him." He held out his hand.

"Brighton McKenzie," he said, shaking the offered hand because it was polite. "Tanner isn't here right now. He took the truck because he said he had some errands he had to run this afternoon."

"You the owner of this place?" Royce looked around. "If you don't mind my saying, it could use some work. It don't look big enough to support anybody." He turned back to Brighton. "You must need help with the place."

Brighton lifted his cane, tempted to wield it as a weapon to knock the self-satisfied look off this guy's face. Yeah, he needed help, and yes, this guy was definitely raised in a barn with no common courtesy whatsoever. "I inherited it recently from my grandfather. This land has been in my family since before the Revolution. It may be small, but I have big plans for it. Now, was there something you wanted other than to hurl insults? Because if not, I'll tell Tanner you were here." Brighton pointed toward the road. "And you can get going."

"I didn't mean to insult you," Royce said. "I'm just used to different."

Brighton was starting to wonder if this guy was stupid, completely oblivious, or both. He definitely had manners that would make their pony, Napoleon, blush. "For not meaning to insult me, you sure did a good job. And I'm wondering if you've spent too much time with cattle and not enough with people. Maybe… you were born in a barn." Brighton glared at Royce, daring him to argue. "I'll tell Tanner you were here."

"Can I leave my number?" He fished around in his shirt pocket. "I been looking for him for a solid week."

"If he's your boyfriend, like you claim, doesn't he have it? And wouldn't he have used it if he were interested?" Brighton saw the first chink in Royce's armor. Granted, this was the kind of man he saw Tanner with. Royce was Marlboro Man handsome—strong, with great eyes. He was also an asshole, but that was probably just Brighton being prickly. Brighton took the card and shoved it into his pocket as Royce got back in his car.

"Like I said, there was a whole hubbub, and things need to be set right. That's why I'm here." He smiled a brilliant, perfect smile. Then Royce tipped his hat and left in a cloud of dust that added another layer to the car.

Brighton was tempted to pull the card out of his pocket and tear it to shreds. But that would be petty, and while Brighton was many things, he didn't want to see himself as petty. There were plenty of unflattering words he'd use to describe himself at this very moment: jealous as hell, green with envy, angry as shit, along with inadequate and insecure. So adding petty to the list was definitely overkill. Brighton went back inside after he saw the car disappear. He checked the time on his phone and got ready to leave. Brianne would be here any minute, thank God. He needed someone to talk to.

"SO THIS so-called boyfriend just showed up?" Brianne asked a little while later, as they pushed carts through the grocery store.

"That's what he said." Brighton looked through the packages of hamburger and placed two of them in his cart. He then went down the case to add some chicken and a package of pork chops to his cart.

"What did he look like?" Brianne paused next to him.

"Exactly like a cowboy from the movies. He even talked like one. Big like Tanner, tan, dark hair, features chiseled out of stone." Brighton didn't want to talk about this anymore and pushed his cart farther down to the dairy case. He added milk and cheese to his cart. "Tanner is better looking than this Royce any day of the week."

"That isn't what you're worried about, is it?" She took a half gallon of milk as well. "You really like Tanner, don't you?"

Brighton stopped and placed both hands on his chest. "I don't sleep with everyone who crosses my path." He'd said that more loudly than he intended and placed his hand over his mouth when he realized what he'd said. He'd kept things with Tanner to himself.

"You dog," Brianne teased. "Doing the nasty with the help." She laughed harder, and Brighton rolled his eyes.

"Don't sound so Victorian. I like him, okay? He's kind and thoughtful. He doesn't seem to care about my leg." Brighton remembered the first time they'd been together up in his room and the way Tanner had cared for his leg. It still sent a jolt of warmth through him. "So, yeah, I like him."

"But what if this Royce is his boyfriend and things are the way he described? Has Tanner said anything about him?"

Brighton shook his head. "Tanner mentioned Royce's name once, but he doesn't talk about what happened before he left the ranch in Montana. Royce said there was some 'hubbub' that he straightened out. Whatever the hell that means."

He continued down the aisle. "Now you're afraid that Tanner is going to go back with this Royce guy?" Brianne asked.

"Why wouldn't he? We've known each other for only a few weeks—less, even. Maybe he and Royce have one of those connections or are soul mates who were separated. Hell, I don't know." Brighton stopped and leaned on the cart. "I don't know anything right now. I keep running through things in my mind, and I keep thinking that maybe I was a rebound... thing. He and Royce had broken up, or he'd left because of this hubbub thing, and the two of us...." He was too heartsick to continue.

Brianne pushed her cart next to his. "You did it again, didn't you?"

"Did what?"

"Jumped in with your heart." She gently stroked his shoulder. Brighton cringed. "Don't do that. It's one of the things that makes you special. If you didn't leap with your heart before thinking, you wouldn't be the brother who put his little sister ahead of himself." She let go of him and stepped around the cart. "You gave me a home on your own as soon as you were old enough because you didn't think our aunt and uncle were good enough or doing enough for me. Mom and Dad had died, and you put your life on hold so I could get an education and make something of myself, and I will. You know that. But everything I accomplish will be because of you." She hugged him. "This is not a conversation we should be having in the Safeway, but who gives a damn. You deserve all the happiness in the world. So stop thinking you're worth less than anyone else because you have a bad leg. That just pisses me off."

"But, Bree, it's what people see."

"So what? That's their problem. And just for the record, if Tanner isn't the guy for you, there'll be another."

Brighton scoffed more loudly than he intended. "Right. Because the world puts out strong guys who are gentle and caring by the ton. Please. Tanner is…." Brighton stopped because if he went on, he'd get maudlin again, and he didn't want that. "He's special, and I jumped in with both feet."

Brianne held up her hands. "You don't even know if this Royce guy is telling the truth. He may be completely delusional and full of shit."

That was true.

"The only person who can tell you what's real is Tanner. So let's finish up here, and I'll take you back. He said he was going to do the evening chores, right?" Brighton nodded. "Then he'll be back in an hour or so." She smacked his rear end. "Let's move it, gimpy." She raced away, and Brighton shook his head. Sometimes she could act like a child. He loved when he saw that. It meant the hardships in their lives hadn't scarred her too deeply, at least not as deeply as they had him. That was a blessing.

Brighton continued down the aisle. He just needed a few dry goods, and he got those before heading to the checkout. He waited in line and placed his things on the belt while the cashier scanned everything. Then he paid and met Brianne at her car. She helped him load everything, and then they drove back to the farm. He didn't see the truck, and Tanner's bike was where he'd left it. Brighton went inside, and Brianne unloaded the backseat.

"Why couldn't we put the stuff in the trunk?" Brighton asked.

"Because it's full." Brianne set a load of his groceries on the counter. "I stopped by Costco the other day, and I haven't had a chance to unload. I was hoping Tanner would help me."

"Tanner? Why?" Brighton began putting things away.

"I got you an air conditioner for down here. I'm tired of melting every time I step into this house. It's too heavy for me to lift, so I was hoping Tanner would help." She grinned at him, and Brighton sighed. "You do enough for me."

"Bree." Over the past year or so, she had done a lot to pay him back for what he'd done for her. There had been times when he was completely helpless, and she'd always been there.

"You had the house wiring fixed, so you might as well be comfortable, especially if this is going to be your home. It needs to feel like home, and an oven is not home."

Brighton was still putting the groceries away when he heard the truck pull up outside. He peered through the window and saw Tanner heading out to the barn.

"I'll go ask if he'll help," Brianne said, and she hurried out the door.

Brighton hoped she didn't say anything about Royce's visit. He was fairly sure she'd keep quiet and let Brighton speak with Tanner first. However, there were times that Brianne's mouth ran away with her. "He's going to help as soon as he feeds and waters,"

Brianne said as she strode into the kitchen, the screen door cracking closed.

She helped him finish and then went outside again. Soon Tanner came in and set a large box on the living room floor. "I hope it fits," Brighton said softly. The box must have just fit in her trunk.

"I measured. It's a high-efficiency unit and should be powerful enough to cool the rooms down here, especially if you close the kitchen door." Brianne stepped back and then walked over to him. She hugged him good-bye. "I have to get home." She smirked a little and then stepped back. "Thank you, Tanner." Then she mouthed, "Talk to him," at Brighton before leaving.

Brighton wanted to yell at her but sat in one of the chairs, out of the way. "Do you need help?"

Tanner looked up from the directions and shook his head. He then went outside, and Brighton heard the truck door close a minute later. Tanner returned carrying Brighton's grandfather's tool kit. He set it on some cardboard and then proceeded to screw some pieces onto the air-conditioning unit. Brighton watched, and Tanner said nothing as he worked.

"Did you find what you needed?"

"Yes. I'll show you wh... when I'm d... done." Tanner got the unit together and then opened the window. He slid the air conditioner in, muscles straining, and then closed the window. Tanner then left the room, and a few seconds later, Brighton heard him working outside. The unit seemed to click into place, and Tanner returned and closed up the areas on both sides of the unit using the plastic slides he'd installed. "We need to wait a little while."

"Okay," Brighton said. He got up to get a glass of tea and brought it to Tanner. His hand shook a little when he handed it to him.

"Thank you," Tanner said.

"You had a visitor today." Brighton took the card out of his pocket and handed it to Tanner. "He said his name was Royce and that he was your boyfriend." Saying the words hurt, but then he and Tanner had never said what they were to each other. Hell, Tanner didn't ever talk about his feelings.

"R... Royce was here?" Tanner set the glass aside.

"Yes. He said that there was some hubbub back home that he needed to straighten out and that he came all this way to find you." Brighton didn't have the guts to ask if Tanner wanted to be found. His heart ached. "Apparently Alicia told him you were here when he called."

Tanner stared at the number, and Brighton tried to read the emotions in Tanner's eyes. He was hoping for anger or for Tanner to fling the card away and then pull Brighton into his arms. But none of that happened.

"I need to go," Tanner whispered.

"I understand," Brighton said as his throat constricted. "If you truly care for him, then you need to see him and find out what he has to say." Tanner stopped and turned toward him. "You need to be with the person who will make you happy, and I won't stand in your way." Royce had so many things that Brighton couldn't offer. He was a cowboy, like Tanner, and looked like the kind of man Tanner should be with. Royce didn't need a cane to get around, and his car, while covered in dirt from his drive, cost more than Brighton made in two years. He'd recognized it as a high-end muscle car, even under the dirt. Royce had everything that Tanner deserved, and if he was what Tanner wanted, then... "You should go and find out what he wants. He obviously cares for you if he came all this way to see you." Brighton turned and walked toward the kitchen. He needed some physical distance. He only hoped his leg didn't give out on him.

Tanner stood up and shoved the cardboard and packing into the air-conditioner box. He hauled it outside, presumably to the trash. Tanner came back inside, and Brighton smiled, leaning against the kitchen doorframe. For a second he hoped Tanner had changed his mind and wanted to stay. Instead, Tanner strode by him and into the kitchen, returning a few seconds later with the letter to take to his cousin. Then Tanner rushed out the front door without turning around. A minute later the throaty sound of Tanner's motorcycle cut the evening air. It revved, and then the pitch changed as Tanner got farther and farther away.

Brighton peered behind him and then sank into the chair. He didn't move much after that for a very long time. He knew he'd given his heart to Tanner and wasn't sure what to do. His phone rang eventually, and he picked it up, hoping it was Tanner.

"What happened?" Brianne asked as soon as he answered.

"I told him about Royce, and he said he had to go." Brighton tried to keep his voice steady but failed miserably. "He couldn't get out of here fast enough." Images of Tanner and Royce together had plagued him for hours.

"Did he say anything at all?" Brianne asked.

"He took the card, stared at it, and said he had to go. Then he cleaned up the box from the living room, carried it out, and left. He didn't say anything else." Brighton sighed softly. "All I can think is that he's still in love with Royce, and I was some kind of rebound guy."

"You don't know that."

Brighton reached over and turned on the air conditioner. It hummed surprisingly softly and began pumping cool air into the room. "Yes, I do. I saw the look on Tanner's face. There was hope in his eyes when he was looking at that card. I know it."

"Brighton, take it easy."

"How can I? Tanner...." Brighton gasped. "Fuck, I messed up everything."

"Hey, this isn't your fault. Sometimes things happen, you know that." Brianne was trying to be comforting, but Brighton didn't want to be comforted. "How could you have messed everything up? Is there something you aren't telling me?"

"It's not that. It's me."

"You need to stay calm and not get too upset. You don't know what happened between Tanner and this Royce guy. They obviously have some sort of history, but Tanner left and ended up here, thousands of miles from Royce, for a reason. His showing up and the way Tanner reacted could have nothing at all to do with you." She sounded so reasonable, but Brighton's chest felt like it was going to implode, and he couldn't get over the way Tanner had simply left.

"He just left. Tanner hasn't left without a little touch or a kiss since… well, in a while. He always says good-bye. But he just turned and walked out without a word or anything."

"Okay," Brianne said gently. "I suggest that you give him a little time. He was supposed to go home tonight anyway, right?"

"Yeah."

"Has he ever not shown up in the morning to take care of the animals?"

"Not since I hired him," Brighton said.

"Then don't worry. He'll probably be back in the morning, and you can talk to him then. And this time really talk to him. Find out what happened and if Tanner needs help. Tell him you want to know because you care and are worried about him." Brianne paused most likely for breath. "You men all think everything just happens and to hell with talking to one another."

"And you're an expert on this because…?"

"I read," Brianne countered.

"Okay, then. Just don't believe everything you read," Brighton countered.

"Yes, sure. Maybe I'll try to get some firsthand experience."

Brighton paused. "Are you seeing someone?" Brianne rarely dated; she'd been too busy these past few years.

"There's a man from one of my classes. He just got his MBA, and he's asked me out. I think I'm going to go and see what happens." The excitement in her voice was plain as anything.

"Then have fun and don't—"

Brianne cut him off. "Please. I'm not a child anymore. Maybe if things work out, I'll bring him by to meet you sometime. But you have to promise not to scare him off."

"You haven't had a date yet, and you're worried about me scaring him off? I think you can do that just fine on your own." Brianne could be intense, and it would take a strong, intelligent man, secure in who he was, to be Brianne's partner. He sincerely hoped she found him, because in his opinion Brianne was too good a person to be alone.

"Har, har. Look I need to go. But try not to let things run away with you, and get some sleep. Tanner is a good person, or you wouldn't care about him the way you do. Just trust that and give him the time he needs."

"I'll try," Brighton promised, but he wasn't sure how well he was going to be able to keep that promise. His right leg shook, and he kept looking out the window whenever he heard what might be a motorcycle on the road. They said good night and disconnected. Brighton got up and sat near the front window so he could see better. He watched the drive for a few minutes and then turned away.

He went into the kitchen and made something quick to eat. The animals were set for the night; Tanner had seen to that. He ended up heating up a frozen microwave meal and stood at the counter to eat because he didn't feel like sitting any longer. Once he was done, he threw away the trash and dumped the dishes in the sink before going outside.

He was restless as hell. His leg didn't hurt, so he walked around the yard a little. The truck was parked on the west side of the house. As he approached it, he wondered why there were leaves sticking out of it. As he got closer, he realized the bed was filled with trees in pots—dozens of them. Brighton wondered where they'd come from. He pulled open the door. A bill of sale sat on the seat from the farm supply. Apparently they had given Tanner a huge discount in some closeout sale, and he'd bought all they had.

Brighton climbed into the driver's seat and stared at the bill. There were apple, pear, and cherry trees. According to the bill, there were peach trees as well. Brighton swallowed hard, wondering what the hell he'd done wrong. "Dammit, Tanner, I wish you'd talked to me."

Tanner had a huge heart, as evidenced by the truck full of trees he'd gotten for him. What hurt most was that he knew Tanner would be better off with someone else, someone who could pull his own weight and wouldn't need help all the time. He sat forward and let his head rest against the steering wheel. He was so fucking tired of being scared all the damn time. Ever since that fucking accident.... Brighton stopped himself. No, it went a whole hell of a lot further back than that. Losing his parents had knocked his legs out from under him. The accident had done the same thing, only physically. Kurt leaving had hurt him, and he'd loved....

This was different. Very different. Yes, he'd loved Kurt. But it hadn't been that deep kind of love that once you have it you can't live without it. He hadn't felt hurt deep down in his soul, not the way he'd felt with Tanner. When they were together, it was like Brighton had found the other part of himself, the piece that had always been missing. Hell, Tanner hadn't even cared about his leg. Tanner had never said it, but Brighton had thought he cared about him—that Tanner might even have loved him in a way Kurt never had.

Brighton lifted his gaze, and all he saw in the rearview mirror was the green reflection of Tanner's thoughtfulness. Brianne was right—all he could do was hope Tanner came back in the morning so they could talk and he could learn what was going on and what Tanner truly wanted. He hoped Tanner wanted him, but he wasn't counting on it. He couldn't. Fuck it, all of this could very well be part of his own insecurity and everything could be fine in the morning. All this soul searching and vacillation was probably for nothing. He just wished Tanner had given him some indication of how he felt.

Brighton got out of the truck. The interior was like an oven, and he needed relief from the heat. He closed the door, and as he passed the bed of the truck, he checked the pots standing in neat rows. The soil was dry, so he walked to the hose, turned on the water, and gave each of them a drink. Tanner had been kind enough to bring them to him, and he didn't want them to die. Once he was done and had turned the water off again, he went to the porch, keeping one eye on the brilliant sunset and the other on the driveway, in case Tanner returned. He didn't, so Brighton eventually went inside and up to bed.

He slept fitfully, waking every hour, thinking he heard something in the house. Not that he actually could over the hum of the air conditioner. When it was time to get up, he dressed and went downstairs, looking out the window at the barn. The door was closed, and nothing appeared to have changed. He checked where Tanner usually parked his motorcycle, but it was empty. Brighton had his answer. It wasn't the one he'd wanted, but what the hell could he do?

He pulled out his phone, made the call he needed to make, and then called Brianne.

"You better be dead, calling me at six fucking thirty in the morning."

"Is that any way to answer the phone?" Brighton countered.

"It is at six 'what the fucking hell' thirty in the morning. This better be good." Definitely not a morning person.

"Tanner isn't here." Brighton kept the hurt and disappointment out of his voice as best he could.

"Did you try calling him?"

"Yeah. There was no answer." He shook his head to no one. "Go back to sleep. I'll take care of things. I'm sorry I called you. I can let the animals out and make sure they have water." That was about the limit of what he could do, but it would do for a day. "I'm sorry I bothered you."

"Brighton, I'll be there as soon as I feel human."

"No. It's okay. Things will be fine for a day or two. I'll figure out what I need to do somehow." He hung up and stepped out the door.

The air had a hint of crispness, unusual for late June. He took a deep breath and then stepped off the porch and made his way across the yard. His leg felt decent, and maybe this was the beginning of the healing and progress the doctors kept saying they were sure was coming. He easily made it to the barn. He used the hose rolled at the far end to fill all the troughs and didn't make too big a mess in the process. He added feed and then opened the doors so all the animals had access to the outside pens.

By the time he was done, he felt pretty good, so on his way back, he grabbed a shovel and headed to the truck. He opened the door and shoved the spade inside. That asshole Royce had pretty much said he was useless. Well, he'd see who was useless, that fucker!

Full of energy, Brighton went back in the house and got the keys to the truck. He thought about eating but wasn't hungry. When he returned he climbed behind the wheel and started the truck. To his surprise he was able to drive it. Not well, but he could control the speed of the truck, which had been what he couldn't do before. He had to use his left foot for the brake, but he was only going to the other side of the property and managed it just fine. He parked beside the area Tanner had turned and got out.

The sun was coming up, and it was already warm, but it felt good to be out on his own property, like his grandfather was there with him, smiling as he worked the land and tried to put it to productive use. He turned off the engine and got out. He walked around to the back and pulled the bed open. It flopped down with a bang, and Brighton began pulling out some of the apple trees.

They were heavier than he expected, but he got them out one by one and sorted the ones left in the bed by type. Then he figured out how he wanted to lay things out and got to work. He figured a small grove of each type of tree would work well. He used lines of the existing trees as a guide and started digging his first hole.

Since the earth had been turned, the first part was easy. As he got down deeper, the earth got harder, but he got the hole dug and put the tree in the hole, then filled in dirt around it. The small trees still had sticks supporting them, and he left them for now and went on to the next hole.

He got six trees planted and was starting on the next hole when the sun went behind some clouds. The humidity kept going up, and Brighton, who'd been sweating up a storm, was grateful for the relief. He was also running out of energy and supremely relieved that he hadn't pulled everything off the truck. He finished the hole for the last apple tree and tamped the dirt around it as best he could. He looked back and smiled. He'd gotten the apple trees planted in two lines, and they looked good. He put the shovel in the back of the truck, then heaved the tailgate closed. His good leg slipped out from under him. Instinctively, he tried to catch himself. Pain shot up through his leg, and he fell to the ground.

"Fuck it all to hell!" Brighton screamed. He tried to stand, but moving hurt like nothing he could remember in months. He shifted to get his knee as comfortable as possible and reached into his pocket for his phone. When he pulled it out he saw the screen was cracked. He tried to call up the program so he could make a call, but the screen remained black. He was right and truly screwed unless he could get into the truck. He crawled on the ground toward the door, feeling like a fish out of water. Each movement made his leg hurt worse.

Thunder rumbled in the distance, and Brighton knew he had to get inside somehow. He used his cane and the truck and tried to get himself up. He finally made it and dragged his useless leg to the door. He opened it and got inside the truck.

Lightning flashed closer. The ground under the truck would turn to mud once the rain started, and then both he and the truck would be stuck. Brighton started the engine and used his left foot to hold the brake. Then he lifted it up, and the truck began to move, slowly. He couldn't give it gas. He tried with his left foot, but it didn't work, and all he ended up doing was goosing it. At least he went a little faster and managed to get the truck out of the field. It rolled up to the house as the first raindrops hit the windshield. He stopped, put the truck in park, and turned off the engine.

The sky opened up, and Brighton realized he wasn't going anywhere. He couldn't get out of the truck between the rain and his leg, which throbbed and pulsed with pain. Using his hands Brighton shifted on the seat and got his leg out in front of him. The pain was excruciating, and he held his breath while he moved it and then breathed a sigh of relief once he was as settled as he could possibly be.

The wind blew the rain against the other side of the truck, so Brighton cracked the windows on his side for fresh air and hoped like hell Brianne decided to stop by, regardless of what he'd told her. Most likely, however, he'd be stuck there for quite a while. The rain continued getting heavier and then eased up, only to pour down once again.

Brighton tried to move as little as possible as the pain in his knee went from a sharp sting to a throbbing ache that went all the way up his leg. He could almost feel his knee swelling. He needed help.

After half an hour, he saw red outside the truck window. Brighton hoped it was someone to help him. The passenger door opened.

"Brighton?" Tanner said, sticking his head inside the truck. "What are you doing out here?"

The rain had finally let up. "I hurt my leg."

"Okay, what d… do you need?"

"I can't walk. My knee's all messed up."

"B… but why are you here?"

Brighton didn't know how to explain. "I'm not helpless."

Tanner climbed inside the truck. "Who said y… you were?" The movement of the car seat sent pain through Brighton's knee.

"Your boyfriend," Brighton retorted. "You need to teach him some manners." Tanner stopped, looking up at him. "When he was here yesterday—I swear, in five minutes he insulted me and the farm, and he looked at me like I was an invalid. He even asked me how I could do anything here." Brighton seethed when he thought about it.

Tanner backed away and closed the truck door. Brighton thought he'd gone, but then he heard a tapping behind him. He shifted slightly, and Tanner opened the driver's door behind him. Tanner climbed in and held him upright. "S… so you decided to what, plant trees? Did that prove you weren't helpless?"

"No. It just confirmed it. I can't do a damn thing around here." Brighton turned and looked outside the door. "Where is your boyfriend, anyway?"

Tanner put his arms around Brighton's chest. "He's right here. Though I'm s… starting to think he isn't as sm… smart as I thought he was. Planting t… trees." Brighton closed his eyes and leaned back against Tanner. He felt like such a fool, trying to prove something to someone. Maybe he'd really been trying to prove something to himself. He wasn't sure, but all he'd really proven was that he was a damned fool.

"But he said…. Royce said that he… that you…."

Tanner held him tighter. "Now who's the one who stutters?" Tanner held him tighter. "When I d… didn't find you in the house, I went looking." Tanner's voice sounded heavy. "You scared me. I th… thought you might be in the barn, but then I saw the truck had been moved. How long have you been in here?"

"About two hours, I guess. I need to get inside," Brighton told Tanner. "We can talk all you want then."

"No. I have to call an ambulance. You need help." Tanner didn't release him, and Brighton felt him quivering slightly.

"Just carry me into the house," Brighton whispered.

"No." Tanner shifted and then pressed a phone into his hand. "Call for help, or I'll call your s… sister." He pointed to the phone. Brighton turned and gasped slightly at Tanner's stern, serious expression.

"You wouldn't," Brighton said, and Tanner nodded forcefully. "Meanie," he teased and made the call to 911. As soon as he hung up, Brighton leaned back against Tanner. His leg hurt worse and worse, throbbing with each beat of his heart. He knew he was in rough shape. "What am I going to do if they have to take my leg?"

"Get a n... new one," Tanner told him.

"You're a big help." Brighton shifted and hissed at the stab of pain. This was bad, really bad. He knew it, and he began to shake. Tanner continued holding him as the sun came out and the air and truck got hotter and stickier. Tanner didn't move, and Brighton drew in the heavy air, sweating like crazy.

Sirens sounded in the distance, getting closer and closer until Brighton saw lights through the foggy windshield. He hoped like hell they'd give him something for the pain—his teeth hurt, he'd been clenching them so hard. "Make sure they don't cut off my leg," Brighton said to Tanner, then the pain overwhelmed him, and he passed out.

Brighton remembered jostling and then pulling to a stop. It all happened on the edges of his consciousness. The pain lessened, and Brighton figured he'd been given something. Thank God.

Then he was moving again, lights flashing overhead. He kept his eyes closed as he came to a stop again. People were talking to him, and he did his best to answer, but he was comfortable, the pain receding, and he didn't want to open his eyes. After a while he was traveling again. His leg hurt when it shook. After rolling through the hallways again, he was back and stayed in one place for a while.

"Mr. McKenzie, can you hear me?"

"Yes," Brighton answered. His eyelids still seemed heavy, but he forced them open and then closed them again. The light was turned down, and he tried again, this time with better results. "I can hear you."

"I'm Dr. Patel, the surgeon. We need to try to fix your knee as soon as possible before the swelling cuts off the blood supply to your lower leg. The nurse will bring you some papers to sign, and then we're going to prep you for surgery. Is that okay?"

"Yes." Brighton rolled his head to where Tanner sat in the chair.

"We called your sister."

"You can tell Tanner what's going on too," Brighton said.

"Very well. The nurse will be in to take care of everything. I want to get started as soon as possible."

"I understand," Brighton slurred. This was all his fault, and he knew it. "Just save my leg."

"I'll do everything I can. I promise." The doctor lightly touched his shoulder and then left. Brighton knew that was doctorspeak for "we'll try to save your leg but can't make any promises." A few minutes later, a nurse came in with the forms he needed to sign, and then the activity around him increased. He said good-bye to Tanner, who squeezed his hand and promised he'd be here when he got back.

At some point Brianne arrived, but Brighton was pretty much out of it by then. Eventually he was wheeled off to surgery, and the last thing he remembered seeing was Tanner's worried expression. Everything after that was a blur. People moved around him, and then he was waking up in recovery.

"You did very well," the nurse said. "Just relax, and don't try to move. In a few minutes we'll get you something to drink. Are you in pain?"

Brighton wasn't, but he figured that was a temporary situation. Sure enough, as the anesthetic slowly wore off, the pain grew. The nurse put something in his IV, and he felt better very quickly. As the pain receded, Brighton closed his eyes.

"It's all right. You're doing well. Are you thirsty?"

Brighton made an affirmative sound, and the nurse placed an ice chip between his lips. It was cold and melty, and it felt good when the water dripped down his parched throat. She stepped away, and Brighton cracked his eyes open. Brianne sat next to him. She gently took his hand.

"You are so stupid," Brianne began.

"I'm in pain. You can berate me later," Brighton mumbled. At least he knew things were relatively normal with his sister.

"Okay, but I intend to do that. What were you thinking?" She continued holding his hand. "You scared both of us half to death." She looked up, and Brighton followed her gaze to Tanner, who sat in the chair a little ways from her. "Deciding you should plant trees. Maybe I'll see if they can examine your head while you're here."

"Thanks for the sympathy," Brighton said.

"Like you deserve any after you did this." She didn't let go of his hand, though, and leaned closer. "I see he came back."

"He saved me," Brighton whispered to her although he wasn't sure how soft his voice actually was. Everything was messed up, and his eyelids were getting heavy again. "Do I still have a leg?"

"Yes. They saved it. You have metal parts now rather than the ones God gave you." She patted his hand. "You're going to be all right as long as you don't try anything like that again."

"Leave it to you to scold me when I'm in pain and recovering from surgery." He shifted his gaze, and Brianne put an ice chip to his lips. He decided he'd done enough talking and closed his eyes. He was going to be okay, and Tanner had come back. That was enough for him for now. He could deal with the rest when the time came.

CHAPTER 6

TANNER SAT in the chair next to Brighton's hospital bed. He'd spent as much time with him as he could. Brianne had taken him home the night before, dropping him at the farm so he could make sure the livestock had been seen to and get his bike. Then he'd ridden home and returned to the hospital in the morning after the feeding and chores. Brighton was still asleep when he walked in the room. Tanner sat in the chair, remaining as quiet as he could.

He sighed to himself as he thought about how Brighton being in the hospital was partly his fault. Clearly the man needed help and support. He could be so independent. But Tanner should have talked to him before he left. He hadn't hurried away because he wanted to get back with Royce. He'd needed time to think, and being around Brighton often meant he couldn't do that. Brighton tended to consume his attention—his scent, seeing him, even the way he leaned on his cane, watching him when he didn't think Tanner knew about it, was exciting. He couldn't remember anyone ever looking at him as though he hung the moon. That in itself was special.

"Did you stay all night?" Brighton whispered from the bed.

"No. I took care of the animals last night and again this morning. I th… think they miss you. Even Napoleon, who usually attacks his morning feed as though he's starving to death, seemed subdued and quiet. I got here just a few minutes ago." Tanner took his hand and made small circles on his fingers. "I sh… should have talked to you before I left."

"So Royce isn't…?"

"Only in his mind," Tanner said.

Brighton turned toward him. "You want to tell me about it?"

136

Tanner looked around. "Here?"

"I'm not going anywhere." Brighton squeezed his hand and then closed his eyes. "You can talk if you want. I'm just resting my eyes."

"How about I tell you once you come home," Tanner said.

"Sounds like you aren't sure how I'll take what you have to say."

Tanner wasn't sure what to think, truth be told. "Royce is the son of the man who owns the ranch I worked on. He's also as gay as they come, but his daddy doesn't know it or didn't know it—I guess he does now." He kept his tone level and tried not to feel nervous. This was Brighton he was talking to, and if he wanted to be close to him, then he needed to tell him the truth. "You know it's h… h… hard for me to talk."

Brighton opened his eyes, turned his head toward him, and gently reached out, cupping Tanner's cheek in his hand. "You never have to be ashamed of anything with me." Brighton looked down at his leg wrapped in bandages. "You accepted me for who I was. I think that was what hurt the most when I thought you were gone. People don't accept others for who they are very often. So if you can accept me, then why would you think I wouldn't accept you?"

"People call me dummy and stupid all the time. They have since I was a kid. No one wants to love someone who's dumb or who they think is dumb."

"You aren't dumb, and you never have to worry about how you sound. Because I want to hear what you have to say."

Tanner let Brighton tug him into a kiss. He straightened up when a throat cleared behind him.

"Okay, boys. You'll have plenty of time for that once you get home." The nurse smiled and pulled the curtain. "I need to check your vitals and make sure you're comfortable. The doctor should be in a little later." She began checking his temperature and then took his blood pressure. "Are you in pain?"

"A little. Less than I thought I would be," Brighton said and did his best not to blush.

Tanner sat back down, but he didn't let go of Brighton's hand.

"That's good." She continued working with the machines, checking Brighton over.

Tanner stayed out of the way, but he didn't let go of Brighton's hand. He wanted to maintain that connection. After their misunderstanding, it was important to him that Brighton know he was there and wasn't leaving.

"So how did you do this to yourself?" the nurse asked.

"He was planting trees," Tanner said. "He knew he sh… shouldn't, but he d… did it anyway."

"Are you going to tell everyone about my stupidity?"

"Until you promise not to do it again, yes." Tanner met Brighton's gaze. He fully intended to make sure Brighton never did anything to hurt himself again. Not if Tanner could help it. That was his new job: to keep Brighton healthy, whole, and happy. It should have been his job before, when he'd started to realize how hc felt about the man lying in the hospital bed.

"You realize you've said more to me already today than you usually do in a whole day." Brighton turned to the nurse. "He's a man of few words."

The nurse paused and looked at Tanner. "My son is a little younger than you, and he stutters too. He doesn't say a lot either, and I think that's wrong. You have a voice just like anyone else, and what you think and have to say is just as important. I can tell you this. I know you don't know me from Adam, but if you don't speak up for yourself, then others will speak for you, and that may not be what you want." She turned away and looked like she thought she might have said too much. "I'm sorry. I tell him the same thing all the time, and sometimes my mouth runs away with me."

Tanner nodded.

"I've said the same sort of thing," Brighton said. "I like the sound of his voice. It's sexy."

Tanner blushed. He didn't mean to, but he couldn't help it. No one had said anything like that to him before.

"They'll bring in breakfast soon, so I'm going to get you ready." She raised the back of Brighton's bed and fluffed his pillows. Then she smiled at Tanner, and he returned it, and then the nurse left the room.

"You rest," Tanner said and watched as Brighton closed his eyes. "You'll feel better soon." He certainly hoped so.

"I'm not going to forget that you owe me an explanation about what happened," Brighton said.

"I feel so stupid," Tanner said.

Brighton pulled his hand closer. "There's nothing stupid about caring for someone and then having your heart stomped."

Tanner caught his breath. "It's not that simple."

"Nothing ever is. But don't feel bad. Royce is gone, right?"

Tanner nodded. "I told him we weren't getting back together and th... that he should go home. He wasn't happy, since he spent days driving here. Well, he *said* he spent days driving here, but the car wasn't one he had before, and there were Georgia plates on it. I think it was a rental or something."

"What about all the dirt that was on it?"

Tanner shook his head. "I don't know. But if he said he drove all the way from Montana, then he would make sure the car looked like it. But I can say I've never seen Royce drive anything other than a truck. So I looked a little closer."

"Did you tell all this to Royce?"

Tanner sighed. "I just told him to go home. That what we had can't be fixed." The words came easily now, without a stutter to be heard. "I'm happy now, and I realized that I wasn't then, even when things were good. So I promise to tell you all about it. But not now." He swallowed hard. "When you get home, I'll tell you everything you want to know." Tanner leaned over the bed to make sure Brighton could see him. "I want you to understand that I did think Royce cared about me. He didn't, though, not enough anyway."

Brighton turned toward him. "I don't understand."

"Let's just s… say that Royce had to have everything on his own terms, and I'm not willing to live my life like that. He isn't like you, willing to listen or take the time to hear what I have to say. Royce moves at one speed: his own." Tanner felt his throat tighten. "When he showed up, I had to get away, and I'm sorry I didn't talk to you before I left."

An orderly came into the room with Brighton's breakfast. He placed it on the tray and wheeled it to where Brighton could easily reach his food.

"You don't have to stop," Brighton said.

"Yes, I d… do. You're more important, and making sure you feel better is what I need to focus on. I don't want to talk about Royce anymore." Tanner had honestly thought he'd left all that behind, and that was where he wanted it to stay. Forever. That pain and disappointment were best left in the past. "Now eat your b… breakfast, and after that you can take another nap."

Brighton huffed softly and began to eat. Tanner had to admit the food looked plain. Brighton mostly picked at it and then lay back. "I don't want any more."

"Okay." Tanner moved the tray back a little, and Brighton closed his eyes. Tanner leaned over the bed. "I'm going to go back to the farm for a while. There are things I have to do, but I'll be back. I promise." He leaned over the bed and kissed Brighton deeply. "You rest."

"Okay," Brighton agreed. He told Tanner about the planting project he'd been working on, and Tanner squeezed his hand one last time and then placed it under the blanket. He turned to leave but stopped at the door, watching Brighton for a few moments before heading down the corridor of the huge medical complex. He made his way out to the parking lot and got in the truck. Then he drove back to the farm. He stopped near the house, where he loaded the trees he'd taken out of the back that morning and headed out to the orchard.

The heat was already building as he started working. Tanner continued the rows Brighton had started, sticking with the overall plan that Brighton had told him about at the hospital.

"I thought I'd find you here," Royce said as he walked across the field toward him.

Tanner was nearly finished, and he wanted to get the last of the trees in the ground and watered. They wouldn't last long in the pots in this heat, which was why he'd gotten them at such a good price. Then he was going to take some pictures, so he could show Brighton when he went up to see him after cleaning up. "What are you doing here?"

"I came to give you one last chance to change your mind," Royce said with one of his patented smiles. It had been the same smile Tanner had fallen in love with, or thought he had. But now it looked fake, and Tanner wondered what Royce was hiding.

"I haven't." Tanner thrust the shovel into the dirt. "It's over, Royce. When I f... first got here, I h... hoped all the time that you would show up."

"I'm here now." Royce stepped closer.

Tanner swallowed. "It's too late," he whispered. "See, I found someone who cares about me as much as I care about him." Tanner left the shovel in the ground and lifted off his hat. He wiped his forehead with the back of his hand and then plunked his hat back down.

Royce was a good-looking man; Tanner couldn't deny that. He had muscles in all the right places, a smile as bright as the sun, and eyes that sparkled. But that's all there was. "It's never too late, you know that." Royce motioned around him. "You'd rather work here at a rundown farm in the middle of the city that's probably going to end up covered by more of those"—he pointed to the condo complex—"when they decide to expand." Royce stepped closer, and Tanner felt the same draw he had when they first met.

Tanner held his ground. "This land has been in Brighton's family for a long time, and he isn't going to leave it without a fight."

"Is that your ammunition? Those few fruit trees that will take ten years to produce a peach? Please." He scoffed dramatically. "You can have everything. You know I'm going to inherit the ranch—all of it. Once Daddy's gone, everything will be mine. Well, ours."

Tanner gaped at Royce. "You are such a f... fucking liar. You know what your daddy thinks of me. He made that perfectly clear, and I know you said you straightened things out, but did you talk to your dad?" Tanner glared, and after a few seconds Royce's gaze shifted. "See? You're full of shit up to your brown eyes."

"My dad doesn't have to know everything. A friend of mine has agreed to take you on at their ranch. They need a good hand, and I explained all about the misunderstanding. They'd be thrilled to have you, and they understand about me, so we can see each other." Royce did that wounded-puppy thing with his lips and eyes that always used to get to Tanner, but it didn't this time. He wouldn't let it. Those looks were all just a ruse to get what he wanted. Royce was a master of that. Hell, Tanner figured there was probably no job. That was just a line, and once Tanner was back in Montana, Royce would say it fell through, and he'd be up a creek... again.

Tanner shook his head. "I know you think I'm dumb. You must to think I'd buy the load of crap you're selling. See, I've got people here who care what I have to say and don't think they have to find jobs for me, or think th... that I'm helpless enough to accept being your d... d... dirty little secret. I'm not." He paused. "Everyone here knows who I am. Arthur does, and so does Alicia, and Brighton loves me enough to accept me for who I am—a cowboy turned farmhand, who doesn't talk so good."

"You're more than that, you're sexy and hot, and...."

"I look good on your arm. That's all you care about and all you ever did. How things look." Tanner stepped forward and snatched the hat off Royce's head. "This cost more than I ever made in a month, and it's just your damned hat." He dropped it on the ground. "It's just a hat and shouldn't require a mortgage to pay for it. I'll never understand why you didn't stand up to your daddy when he was so down on me. Why'd you let him do all that to me? Now I know. It was that damned hat." Tanner kicked dirt toward it, and Royce scooped it up, brushing it off before placing it on top of his perfect haircut.

"So this is it? You're choosing this over me and all the good times we could have had?" The disbelief in Royce's eyes told Tanner he still didn't get it, and he probably never would. "I can have the pick of anyone I want—boys, girls, anyone—and I want you."

"Well, I suggest you return that rental car after you wash off the crap you put on it, get on a plane, and when you get home, tell your daddy to start lining up fillies for you to marry. You can have your pick of any of them, so choose. C... c... cause I'm not in the lineup no longer. I'm choosing someone who cares about me over you, and someone who will p... p...." The simple word caught in his throat.

"Put," Royce said.

"I know, asshole," Tanner snapped. "Put me first and not act like a condescending buttwad. I stutter. So fucking what. You always look at me like I'm dirt under your feet when I stutter. Brighton never has. He's patient and kind, and he cares about me." Tanner jabbed his chest. "I know he does." Tanner stepped forward and popped Royce on the jaw. Royce wasn't expecting it and went down on his ass. "That's for insulting this farm and for saying that Brighton was useless." Tanner rubbed his knuckles. He'd only hit one other person in his life, and that was in the tenth grade, when one of the bullies was teasing another kid. "I suggest you stay there for a while, or I'll break your nose next time."

"This Brighton sounds like a real man's man, all touchy-feely." The way Royce raised the pitch of his voice made Tanner see red.

"A real man doesn't need all this shit, and let me tell you something, Royce Weston. Brighton is more of a man than you'll ever be... in every way possible." Tanner stared at him. "He's strong in the way it really counts, and believe it or not, he's going to make something of this farm. And I'd rather be here with him than with you on that big, fancy ranch your daddy owns. So go home to your big ranch and your bigass truck and huge horse. But know you ain't fooling anybody." Tanner wagged his pinkie at Royce. "Now I suggest you go. You said your piece, but I ain't buying the lies you're peddling. You and your daddy want to have what looks like the perfect life, and you want me or some other piece of ass on the side. Well, go find someone else to be part of your plans." Tanner pointed toward Royce's car, parked back near the house. "I'm sorry you came all this way to have your ass handed to you. You could have called, and I would have done it over the phone just as easily. But now you know how you treated me."

"I won't be back. My offer isn't going to be repeated."

"I'm not a used car," Tanner shouted. "And this isn't *Let's Make a Deal*. You're supposed to care about me, not act like I'm one of your toys." Tanner stood firm, feeling better about his decision with every passing second.

"I'm warning you...."

"Just go before you make a bigger fool of yourself," Tanner told him. "You sound like the character in a bad teenage romance movie." Tanner pointed at Royce. "You'll be sorry. This isn't over," he mocked. Then he grinned. "I'll get you, my pretty, and your little dog too." He did his best impression of the Wicked Witch of the West from the *Wizard of Oz*. Then he laughed full-on. "Go home to Daddy, and let him dictate your life and who you can marry. I'm through letting that wretched, bitter old asshole dictate my life, and when you get tired of the same thing, you'll be a better man and one worth having. But I don't need you...." Tanner watched as Royce finally got the message and stalked back to his car. Tanner saw him get inside and then drive away. He smiled and breathed a sigh of relief.

He leaned on the shovel, using it to help prop himself up. He'd burned that bridge but good. Granted, it was a bridge that needed burning. He'd never had any intention of going back to Montana—with

Royce or anyone else. This was starting to feel like home, and maybe if he asked Brighton, they could get a horse for him to ride. He'd love that. Maybe they could put in a paddock. He could ride across the back of the property and out under the power lines, where they bisected the condominium complexes farther back.

He cleared all those daydreams away and went back to work, getting the last few trees in the ground. Then he pulled one of the bags of limestone pellets out of the truck and sprinkled some around the base of each of the trees. He'd researched and found out that Brighton had been right—fruit trees wanted sweet soil. So the limestone pellets spread on the ground would slowly dissolve with the rain and improve the soil. He ended up spreading two bags and then stood back to survey his work. It looked good. He pulled his phone out of his pocket and took a few pictures before shoving the tailgate back into place and driving to the house.

Grateful Brighton had given him a key, Tanner got some water and made sure everything was okay. He wondered if Brighton might like his computer but decided to leave it where it was. He needed to rest, not work right now.

Once he was sure the house was fine, Tanner locked up and rode his bike home to his cousin's house.

Marky and Josh raced outside as soon as he pulled in the drive. "Can we go for a ride?" Marky asked hopefully. He was a sweet kid but precocious as hell.

"Boys," Alicia called from the front door, but they weren't going to be sidetracked.

"I need to visit Uncle Brighton at the hospital. He got hurt, and he's up there all alone. But I'll give you both a ride really soon."

"Pwomise?" Josh asked, and there was no way he could say no to that sweet face.

"I promise."

"Boys, come inside for lunch," Alicia called. "Have you eaten today at all?" she added to him in the same tone she'd used with the boys.

"Didn't get a chance," Tanner said. He was in a hurry and figured he'd get something at the hospital.

"Then come inside. I made extra. It's just mac and cheese, but it'll fill you up." She shooed the boys inside, telling them to wash their hands. "It looks like you're wearing half the farm."

Tanner looked down at his clothes. "I guess I am. I'll sh... shower and come right back."

"Of course," she said gently. "Just make it fast. Marky and Josh haven't seen you much lately, and they're pretty excited." She went inside, and Tanner hurried up to his room. He stripped and jumped into the shower, then washed and dried off in record time. He dressed and made sure everything was hung up before leaving his room and heading down to the main house.

Marky and Josh sat on stools at the counter. They were clearly waiting for him. Tanner sat at the third stool, and Alicia chuckled as the three of them waited for their lunch. At least he got a proper plate, where the other two got plastic, but he still felt like one of her boys, especially when he got a glass of milk just like the other two.

"Daddy drinks beer," Marky said and made a face that clearly told Tanner he'd tasted some and that it was the worst stuff in the world.

"Don't stick your tongue out," Alicia scolded him gently. "Finish your lunch, and we'll go to the park while Uncle Tanner goes to the hospital."

"Is Uncle Brighton going to be okay?" Josh asked. "I like his sheeps."

"He is. He got hurt, but he'll b... be okay." That seemed good enough for Josh, because he went back to eating.

"Can we see the goats and pony when we go for a ride on your cycle?" Marky asked.

"That's a little f... far to go. But I th... think you can visit the animals whenever your mom wants to bring you over." Tanner looked to her. "In fact, you c... could probably help us." An idea flashed in his mind.

"How?" Alicia asked.

He explained about the zoning hearing and what it would do to Brighton. "Arthur is working on it, but we may need some unconventional help." Tanner wanted to talk it over with Brighton before he did anything else.

"We'll do anything we can. You know that." She smiled, and the boys nodded enthusiastically.

TANNER FINISHED lunch and then said good-bye, getting a hug from each of the boys. Josh hung on until Tanner agreed to swing him. He giggled as Tanner pressed him right up near the ceiling and then swooped him down to the floor. With the boys happy, Tanner left and rode back up to the hospital.

He heard voices as he approached Brighton's room. Arthur sat in the chair next to Brighton's bed. He stood and hugged Tanner lightly.

"Are y... you talking strategy for the hearing?" Tanner asked. He noticed the IV as well as the machines had been removed. Brighton also looked a lot less pale than he had just a few hours earlier.

"Yes," Brighton answered. "It's in a few days."

"D... do you want me to leave?" Tanner was ready to turn back toward the door. If Brighton needed privacy, then....

"No." Brighton held out his hand. "We're trying to figure out what we need to do."

Tanner took it and stood near the bed.

"Basically, the city can do what it wants when it comes to setting up zoning," Arthur said. "However, there is a process that has to be followed. They've set up rules, and they have to follow them, as do we. One of those rules they stated in the letter. There isn't very much farmland in the city. In fact, this could be some of the last. There's a huge history of people requesting that land be rezoned for development, but there isn't a lot of history with the city initiating the rezoning on their own. Mostly, zoning is changed when an owner requests it, and they have to have a very definite reason. The city also can't just change zoning anytime it wants, according to their own rules. Do you see?" Arthur looked at Brighton, whose eyes looked to be spinning in circles.

"I think you need to tell me in plain English," Brighton said.

Tanner had thought the same thing but kept quiet.

"They are basing their rezoning plan on their perception and belief that the farm hasn't been actively farmed in over ten years. They may think they're safe in that assessment because the plot of land isn't large enough for a commercially viable farm."

"So, what do we do?" Brighton asked.

"We attend the hearing and present evidence that the land has been farmed. What would be helpful would be pictures showing recent farming activity. That would make them reset their clock, and a lot of this could go away. You also have the animals that were on the farm when you inherited it. That's additional evidence. But the thing is with these boards, they can be political, and small-city politics will drive a normal person crazy. Each person has their own agenda, and I haven't been able to find out who is really behind this push to have the zoning changed."

"I think it was my aunt," Brighton said.

"Vera?"

"Yes. Didn't I tell you what was said at the funeral?"

"I think so. But she can't make a petition to have the zoning changed. She has to have standing, and she doesn't." Arthur opened his bag and drew out some papers.

"But...," Tanner began. "What if she got a friend to have the city d... do it?" He hated speaking up like this in case he sounded dumb. "She has a reason...."

"Do you really think she would go to these lengths to try to force you to sell?" Arthur drew out more papers from his bag.

"I think she'll do what she thinks she has to to get what she wants." Brighton turned to him. "The one I feel sorry for is Uncle Raymond. She steamrolls over him and has for years." Brighton's eyes drooped, and he lay back on the pillow. It looked like he was tiring. "What exactly should we do?"

"Take pictures of the farm. Show that the buildings are in good repair and that the place isn't falling down. Take pictures of what you're doing and especially what was there when you inherited the property. If you can find receipts for purchases, or better yet the sale of any produce or any farm products, that would help. As I said, these boards tend to be a little haphazard, so we'll beat them over the head and try to knock the leg they're basing this change on out from under them."

"What happens if we lose?"

"We can appeal to the entire city council and ultimately take it to court. But that's drawn-out and messy, and in the meantime they can assess taxes at the higher rate." Arthur consulted the papers he had in his hand. "We want to end this right here and now. I think we have a very good chance of winning this."

"Will you be there?" Tanner asked, concerned that Brighton was getting too tired.

"Yes. I'll be there with him."

"Do you think he can go?" Tanner shifted his gaze down to Brighton, who was now half-asleep and would be out in a few minutes.

"I don't know."

"I'll get there somehow," Brighton whispered and opened his eyes. "Come hell or high water, I'll be there. Think about it: I'll probably be in a wheelchair. That should be good for something."

"It may not. The board could see that as proof that the land won't really be farmed in the future because you're going to be laid up and that the only reason you're fighting this is to reduce what they will see as a fair tax rate. Farmland has a lower tax rate, and the city wants as much tax revenue as they can get."

"That's...." Brighton sat up. "I want to preserve my family's legacy. This is all I have left of my family, of Grandpa. They're trying to take it away from me."

Tanner gently got him to lie back down.

"I'm not saying I agree with them, just what they may think," Arthur said gently. "We need to be prepared for everything and not take anything for granted." Arthur's expression told Tanner that he hadn't meant to upset Brighton. "Relax, and try to get some rest. We have a few days yet, and we'll all need to be strong and thinking clearly if we're going to win this here and now."

"But what if we lose?" Brighton asked.

"Then we'll appeal."

Brighton sighed. "Maybe I should just sell." He closed his eyes like he was trying to retreat from everything. Tanner glanced up at Arthur, flashing a half smile.

"I'll see you later," Arthur said after he'd put everything back in his briefcase. "Like I said, try not to worry. I know it's hard, but we're going to put up the best case we can. It will be a strong one." He smiled as Brighton turned toward him. "I can't guarantee success, but we'll give it one hell of a fight."

Brighton nodded, and Arthur glanced at Tanner and then turned to leave. "Thank you," Brighton said.

"I'll see you soon." He left the room, and Tanner walked around the bed and sat in the chair Arthur had vacated.

"He's trying to help, the same as the rest of us." Tanner sighed. "You need to st... stop talking like that. I know you don't want to sell, but you bring it up every time the going gets rough."

"So?" Brighton snapped.

"So, stop it!" Tanner retorted. "Making a living off the land is hard work. Your grandpa knew that, and he must have thought you were up to the task, or he wouldn't have left you the land. He would have simply let it be sold, and that would have been that. He didn't. So quit whining, get better, and fight this thing."

"Is that what you did? Back in Montana?"

Tanner swallowed. "No. I was pushed around, and I let them do it." He sat back. "Royce's dad owns the ranch I worked on."

He figured he might as well get this over with now that he'd started. "I liked Royce. He was attractive, and he seemed to like m... me." Brighton rolled his head on the pillow until he faced Tanner. He extended his hand, and Tanner took it. "We danced around each other for quite a while, and eventually Royce made the f... first move."

"Did you love him?"

"I thought I did, I guess." Tanner didn't smile. It was funny, but the warm feelings that had been there once now seemed cold and mechanical. "He and I would get together, and we'd... well, we had sex... a lot. He said he loved me, but now I don't really think he did. Not really." Tanner tried to explain. "See, his daddy found out about us, and he fired me on the spot, calling me everything you c... c... can think of." Those words still rang in his ears. "The venom...."

"I'm sorry," Brighton whispered.

"I left and found a small place in town, hoping to get another job or just leave, because it became plain real fast that none of the ranchers wanted a f... f... fag working for them. So I was getting ready to leave when I got a v... visit from the sheriff. Royce's dad said that I had corrupted Royce and suggested that I'd raped him." Tanner could barely breathe, and he turned away.

"My God. Did they arrest you?"

"No. I don't think the sheriff believed him, but when I denied it...." Tanner gasped for breath. "He was none too nice about it and basically said I should get out of town before someone decided to take matters into their own hands." Tanner tried not to recall the look of complete disdain the sheriff displayed. Fat, smelly old fuck.

"Jesus. Does stuff like that really still happen?"

"Yup. He even mentioned that it would be a shame if something like Matthew Shepard happened in town." Tanner's blood had run cold. "I waited one more day, holed up in the dingy motel with my bike parked in back under an old tarp so no one would see it. I hoped Royce would come, but he d… d… didn't. No one d… did. So I packed up and got ready to leave town."

Brighton squeezed his hand. "I take it that isn't all of it?"

"No. I saw Royce on my way out of town. He was driving in as I was going out. I stopped to see what he had to say. He just kept going. He saw me—he admitted he did when I first saw him here—but… he turned his back on me." Tanner took a deep breath. The betrayal and pain that had consumed him roared back to life. Brighton continued holding his hand and lightly rubbed his arm.

"You don't have to go on if you don't want to."

Tanner shook his head. He needed to get this whole thing out so he could be done with it. He was through with Royce, and he needed to be through with this too. "I knew then it was over, and I needed to get away. I'd gone about a mile when a truck came from the other direction. It was filled with men from the ranch. I saw another coming up behind me. The one in front slowed and then turned sideways to block my path. This was what the sheriff had said was coming. I wasn't sure if Royce had called to say where I was or not, but I gunned it and shot around the back of the truck. I nearly fell over but stayed upright and got past. One of the men swung a bat at me, but I ducked and shot by." His heart raced, and Tanner gasped for air as the agitation and terror filled him once again. "I went as far as I could and tried to get a job, but Royce's dad's reach is long. Eventually, out of desperation, I called Arthur, and he told me to come here. I don't think he knew what to make of what happened, but he agreed to help." Tanner was surprised he'd managed to get all that said without stumbling all over his words.

Brighton shifted, and Tanner helped him sit up. "What did that asshole want when he came back, then? That shit said he was your boyfriend." Brighton kept his voice low, but his anger filled the room. "Some boyfriend."

"He said he straightened things out with the men at the ranch as well as the sheriff and had found me a job at one of the ranches. I think I told you that. Maybe I didn't." It was hard for him to remember. His mind seemed all over the place. "Of course, he didn't stand up to his daddy, though. I was supposed to be his little secret until his daddy died and left him everything. Once that happened, life was supposed to be all hearts and flowers shooting out our asses."

Brighton laughed and then groaned but started laughing again. "See, you can talk and say whatever you want." He pulled Tanner's hand to his lips and kissed it. "Snarky becomes you."

He wasn't sure about that, but it was nice that he'd been able to say what he wanted. "I guess it means…."

Brighton tugged him closer. "I know exactly what it means." Brighton kissed him. "And you should always say what you mean."

"I did. I went off on Royce yesterday and sent him home. I think I know what love is now, and it isn't the crap Royce was dishing out." He kept all the hateful things Royce had said about the farm and Brighton to himself. Royce was a spoiled child, and he could be an ass when he didn't get what he wanted. "I think I was just another plaything to him, like a toy. He has a lot of them, gifts from his dad, and he wasn't about to hop off the gravy train, for me or anyone else."

"So he's gone?" Brighton asked.

"I think so. He isn't coming back. No matter what Royce wants to think or tells the sheriff or the other men in town, his daddy is going to have every girl lined up. He knows Royce isn't as straight as he'd like to think." Tanner paused, suddenly realizing he hadn't tripped over his words once. It had been a long time since that had happened.

"Why didn't you tell me this earlier?" Brighton asked. "I knew something had happened—that was clear from the way you acted."

"At first I wasn't sure how you'd react, and th… then…." Tanner felt his throat close and the words stick. "I was ashamed. I cared for Royce. I thought I loved him, and he treated me like shit. So maybe that's what I was, and...." Tanner stopped and took a deep breath, steadying himself. He wasn't going to act like some schoolgirl about this.

"Don't go all stoically quiet on me. Not now." Brighton patted his hand and then leaned back in the bed and closed his eyes. "But then again, you probably will anyway."

"Afternoon," a woman said as she breezed into the room. Brighton didn't move, and Tanner got the distinct feeling he was playing possum. In fact, he knew he was by the slight groan. "It's time for us to take another little walk."

"Walk?" Tanner asked, shocked. "He just had surgery on his knee." He wondered why she had a wheelchair with her.

"Yes. He did, and he needs to get up and get moving." She was young, rather pretty, and energetic, with dark hair and eyes. Tanner guessed she was a popular girl.

"The doctor replaced my knee with a titanium one, and this... woman keeps pestering me to get out of bed and walk." Brighton pushed back the covers. "The least they could do if they want me to get up is give me some clothes so I don't flash my ass at everyone."

"But it's a nice ass," Tanner said softly.

"We had to beat them off with a stick yesterday," the therapist said with a smile. "Don't worry, I brought you some scrub pants, and I'll help you get them on. Then we can go. I'm taking you down to therapy so we can get you moving, teach you to use your crutches, and move that new knee. It will be some time before you can bear your own weight, but we need to move the leg and make sure the muscles don't seize up. I'll also fit you with a brace that will help in healing and prevent reinjury. You want to be able to go home, don't you?"

"God, yes," Brighton retorted. "By the way, Tanner, this ball of sadistic energy is Amanda. She was in here earlier threatening me with this torture." Brighton sat on the edge of the bed, and Tanner took the scrubs and helped Brighton into them.

He wasn't particularly keen on letting anyone help Brighton with his pants. That would be his job.

"Do you need him in the chair?" Tanner asked, turning to Amanda. She nodded, and Tanner carefully lifted Brighton off the bed and set him gently in the wheelchair. "Should I wait here?"

"We'll be about an hour. I would suggest getting some lunch if you haven't eaten already." Amanda wheeled Brighton out of the room, and Tanner settled in the chair beside the bed. After a few minutes he decided that while he didn't need to eat, something to drink would be nice, so he headed down in search of coffee.

He found it. The stuff was dreadful, but he drank it anyway and then returned to the room. Brighton wasn't back yet, so he settled in the chair to wait.

He heard Brighton yammering before Amanda delivered him to the room, so he figured it must not have gone too badly.

"She says that I should be much better than before, and that once this new knee heals, I could be back to normal." Brighton actually sounded chipper. Amanda helped Brighton use his crutches to get back in bed.

"Is that true?" Tanner asked.

A man knocked on the doorframe and then came in the room.

"Let's ask him," Brighton said. "Thanks for all the help, Amanda."

"You're welcome," she said and waved as she wheeled the chair out of the room.

"Ask me what?" the doctor said as he consulted his wheeled computer cart.

"She s... said that his knee would be as good as or better than before," Tanner said to the doctor.

"Better, most definitely. I'm not sure why your knee wasn't replaced after the accident. You would have had a much better recovery."

"They said I was too young," Brighton answered.

"For a normal knee replacement, yes. This one is extra heavy duty and should last thirty years. At that point, you might need another one, but then I've seen these replacements last indefinitely. The important thing is that you should recover the full use of your leg now and be in a lot less pain." He checked Brighton's bandages and the fit of the brace. "I think we can let you go home tomorrow provided you have someone who can stay with you. No stairs for a few days, until you're secure on your crutches. I want you to have one more physical therapy session here in the hospital, and most definitely no tree planting until next spring."

Tanner agreed with that. "I planted them already, in case he g... got any ideas."

"This is my boyfriend, Tanner," Brighton said. "He's the one responsible for the trees in the first place."

"I didn't tell you to try to plant them," Tanner countered, shaking his head. Brighton reached out to him, and Tanner took his hand.

"I don't see any reason you shouldn't make a full recovery. The healing process is going to be slower than with a regular knee replacement because of the condition of your leg and knee in the first place, but the team and I were able to repair some longstanding damage, and hopefully we've given you a knee that will allow you to walk for decades."

"Thank you," Brighton said. "Who would have thought there would be an upside to planting those trees?"

Tanner growled at him but said nothing.

"You were lucky, Mr. McKenzie. Very lucky." The doctor shook both their hands and then left the room.

After the way he'd found Brighton in the truck, Tanner knew that was the best news possible. He had expected the prognosis to be so much worse. "I need to go," he said. There was lots of work he needed to finish on the farm. "I'll come back after the evening feeding." He smiled and leaned over the bed.

"I can't wait to get out of here," Brighton whispered, and Tanner followed his gaze to a very prominent bulge in the bedding.

"B... be good," Tanner said with a smile and kissed Brighton good-bye. "You'll be home tomorrow." It was exciting that Brighton really wanted him. But Tanner wondered for how long.

CHAPTER 7

BRIGHTON WAS ready and waiting the following day when Brianne and Tanner came to bring him home. She had offered to let him stay with her for a few days, but Brighton just wanted to go home. The farm was home now—he felt it deep inside—and once Brianne pulled into the drive with Tanner following in the truck, a sense of peace came over him. When the car had pulled to a stop, he opened the door and waited to be handed his crutches before getting up on them.

"Where are you going?" Brianne demanded.

"You're turning into one bossy pain in the ass, you know that?"

"I learned from the best." She pushed the door closed. "And you didn't answer my question." She hurried behind him. Brighton heard the truck door slam closed, and then Tanner strode past and to the barn door. He pulled it open, and Brighton used his crutches to go inside.

"I want to see the animals," he finally answered as he moved close to Napoleon's stall. The pony stuck his head out and nuzzled Brighton's lower chest and belly. "I know. I missed you too." If anyone had told him a few weeks ago that he would be pleased to have a pony slobber all over him, he wouldn't have believed it. After greeting the pony, he looked in on all the others. "Is she getting fat?" he asked, looking carefully at one of the sheep. "Are we feeding her too much?"

"No. She's pregnant," Tanner said with a smile. "I suspect your grandfather had her bred a few weeks before he died. We have a couple pregnant goats as well. So it looks like spring is coming a little late this year, but we're, I mean, you're going to have some additions."

Brighton caught the change and wondered what caused it. The animals wouldn't be cared for if it wasn't for Tanner. He wondered if that was a symptom of the whole Royce thing, and he wished he had beaten him with his cane when he'd had the chance.

"You should go inside before you get too tired. You had surgery just a few days ago, and I'm sure the doctor didn't mean for you to go traipsing around the farm as soon as you got home," Brianne scolded. "He also said you weren't to go up and down stairs for a few days, until you were proficient on the crutches."

"For gosh sake, quit the nagging," Brighton half teased. "I heard what he said, and you don't need to turn into my mother all of a sudden." He headed toward the door but faltered at the porch steps. Tanner caught him and scooped him up into his huge arms. Brighton leaned against his massive chest and inhaled the scent he loved best in the world. Tanner carried him to the door, and Brianne followed with the crutches.

Brighton worked his hands around Tanner's neck. He didn't want to let go. Brianne hurried past them and unlocked the door with the new set of keys he'd given her. Tanner carried him inside and gently set him on the sofa.

It was hot and stuffy in the house. Brianne turned on the air conditioner, and soon it was blasting cool air into the room. It would still take a while to get the room comfortable, but he was happy to be home.

"I'll run home and get some things so I can spend a few days here," Brianne said.

Brighton looked at Tanner.

Tanner spoke up. "I'll stay with him."

Brianne paused. "Are you sure? Neither of you seems to be able to make anything other than sandwiches."

"I can grill," Tanner countered, and Brianne took a small step back.

"If you're sure, I know he'd rather have you here than me." She smiled. "If you make a list of things you need me to get, I'll run to the store, because chances are all Brighton has in the refrigerator is mayonnaise, ketchup, and cold cuts."

"You don't need to be mean. I have mustard too."

"Okay, then." She rolled her eyes. "Get a list together quick, and I'll go shopping and then leave you two alone to... God, do whatever it is you do. I don't want you telling me. But if you get any more spacey looking...." She leaned over the sofa and kissed Brighton on the cheek. "I'll give you a few minutes to get your list together." Brianne left, and a few seconds later, Brighton heard her hauling the vacuum cleaner upstairs.

Tanner stared at the empty doorway quizzically. "She can't sit still for more than five minutes, so she's probably going to work in one of the upstairs bedrooms. Who knows?" The truth was he didn't care. Brighton tugged Tanner down until their lips met. Instantly he was hard and moaning softly. He'd missed this both because of the misunderstanding and then his injury. But now Tanner was here with him.

The hum of the vacuum cleaner stopped, and Tanner backed away. "The list."

Brighton reached for the pad on the table and began writing things down. "Steaks, potatoes, ice cream, corn, pork chops, stuff for salad...."

"Why all this?" Tanner asked.

"You said you could grill, so this is all the stuff you need to go with grilled food," Brighton said as he added sandwich fixings and some frozen food they could cook in the microwave. "Anything else?"

"Mac and cheese?" Tanner suggested, and Brighton put it on the list. He thought of a few more things, and when Brianne came back down he handed her the piece of paper and some money.

"I'm glad you have something healthy on this list," she said as she headed for the door. "I'll be back in an hour." She hurried out, and Brighton looked up at Tanner, waiting for the sound of her car to fade in the distance. Tanner stood up and locked the front door, then turned toward him with a very heated look. He sat on the edge of the sofa, and Brighton carefully moved his legs over, making room for him. The room was finally cooling. Tanner leaned closer. Brighton put his arms around his neck and pulled Tanner into another kiss, this one deepening fast.

Tanner vibrated with excitement. "You have to promise me you'll stay still and not move."

Brighton pulled back to look in Tanner's eyes. "Okay."

Tanner stood and slipped his hand beneath Brighton's shirt. His stomach fluttered at the gentle touch, and he inhaled, holding his breath. When Tanner reached for his belt, he gasped and closed his eyes, praying and hoping. Tanner seemed to hear him because he tugged open Brighton's pants.

"We need to get you some shorts," Tanner said. He pushed his hands down into Brighton's underwear and wrapped his fingers around his cock as soon as it sprang free.

Brighton moaned and thrust his hips upward, trying to get more friction. He wanted so badly. "Tanner."

Words weren't forthcoming. Instead Tanner leaned forward and sucked him into his mouth. Oh God, that was hot and special. Just what he needed. Brighton had spent days longing for Tanner's touch. He needed him, and fuck if he wasn't getting what he wanted and more.

There was no subtlety. Tanner poured energy and enthusiasm into each movement. He sucked Brighton deep and held still, his throat working his cock.

"Jesus," Brighton moaned, drawing out the word and ending at a near scream as he was sucked within an inch of his sanity. He placed his hands on Tanner's head but did his best not to thrust like a maniac, even though every cell of his being urged him to. It had been so long, and this was absolute heaven on earth. After all he'd been through, Tanner's hot mouth around him was almost more than he could take. "I'm not going to last."

Tanner mumbled something that Brighton didn't understand, but whatever it was vibrated up his cock and shook his very core. Brighton worked to control his breath, letting his head fall back against the arm of the sofa as Tanner stretched his hand under his shirt, tweaking his nipples. Brighton thought Tanner was trying to suck his brains out through his dick, and he damn near succeeded. He might have if Brighton wasn't already tingling from head to toe. Forget about his knee—he couldn't feel his legs as the pressure built to epic levels. He tried to warn Tanner he was close, but his climax hit him like a freight train, and all he could do was hold on and ride it out. Brighton gasped as he shot time and time again down Tanner's talented, sweet throat. Fuck, this was worth all the pain from the injury and the hours wondering if Tanner was coming back.

He collapsed back on the sofa, spent and exhausted. He could barely see straight. Tanner sat on the edge next to his legs, and Brighton tugged him closer. He needed to feel him and know that Tanner was real. The past three days had been tough, Brighton sighed, keeping his eyes closed because it took too much effort to open them. "Just give me a minute," he whispered.

Tanner stroked Brighton's cheek, gentle and caring, but said nothing. "You sleep," he said softly and then stood up.

"But... what about you?"

"I'm fine." Tanner leaned down and kissed him.

"I love you, Tanner," Brighton whispered, as if it might be the wrong thing to say. "I realized it when I kept pushing the curtains aside to see if you had come back. I thought I'd lost you." Some of the misery he'd felt came rushing back. He opened his eyes and stared at Tanner just to convince himself that he was still here and hadn't gone anywhere.

Tanner looked back at him and then hoisted Brighton off the sofa. Brighton curled against his chest and closed his eyes. "Where are we going?" Hell, his pants were still mostly open, and he felt completely debauched. Who cared where they were going as long as Tanner was taking him there?

"Up to bed," Tanner answered and then turned and carried him up the stairs.

"You don't have to carry me everywhere." Brighton chuckled. "I do have legs, and I can walk with the crutches." Tanner didn't answer, so Brighton gave up for now. They'd reached the top of the stairs, and Tanner took him to his room and nudged the door closed. He laid him on the bed and then turned on the air conditioner. The room was stiflingly hot since the heat in the house made its way upstairs during the day. Brighton closed his eyes and waited for the air to cool. It took a few moments, but soon the unit had the heat on the run.

When he opened them again, he was treated to the sight of Tanner's belly and then chest emerging from his shirt as he pulled it over his head. Few men could stretch fabric to the ripping point the way Tanner did. "Sometimes I think you're the Incredible Hulk in disguise." He certainly looked like him—well, with golden, tanned skin that Brighton always longed to touch. Tanner turned around, giving Brighton a good look at his jeans-clad rear end. His belt buckle jingled slightly, and then Tanner bent over, sliding the denim down his legs and treating him to the view of his bare ass just inches away. Brighton would have lunged and buried his face between those perfect, firm cheeks, but Tanner was a little too far away, and he had to be content with the view… for now.

Tanner had forgotten to take his boots off, and Brighton smiled but said nothing when Tanner hopped a little to get them off, along with his socks, and then step out of his jeans. Then he turned around in all the glory nature had given him. "Hulk horny," Tanner said, and Brighton lost it, laughing so hard he could barely see straight.

Tanner joined him, laughing as well. It felt good, but the chuckles died away when Tanner climbed on the bed. Instantly they both had other ideas, and once Tanner was beside him, Brighton, who had been too enthralled with Tanner's striptease to remove his clothes, got out of them with Tanner's help.

The brace made things clumsy, as did the way he had to lie to be comfortable, but Tanner took it all in stride, and once Brighton pressed up against Tanner, everything seemed to fall into place. His hands soothed the worry about the zoning hearing, and his lips kissed away the other concerns. "I love you too," Tanner whispered into his ear.

"Did you love Royce?"

"I thought I did, but not like this." Tanner held him closer. "I th... thought I loved him because he made me feel good. But you make me feel good about being me." Tanner shifted his upper body, and Brighton rested back on the mattress. Tanner kissed him gently at first, but heat built until Brighton was willingly and passionately devoured. "You love me for me."

"And you love me for who I am," Brighton said. Tanner nodded. "Gimpy leg and all."

"Your leg is part of you, just like my stutter is part of me. Your leg will heal, and my st... stutter will get better."

"I don't care if your stutter ever changes, as long as you talk to me and I get to hear the voice that melts my butter."

"That's why it will get better," Tanner said with conviction.

Brighton ran his hands over Tanner's bare cannonball shoulders and along his traps to his neck, locking his fingers behind his head. "For now I think there's a little too much talking and not enough moaning, groaning, and kissing."

Tanner instantly fixed that situation.

THINGS WERE a little awkward, but that didn't dim their ardor or enthusiasm for each other. Tanner's skin tasted heavenly, musky, perhaps even more so now that Brighton knew he was his. The absence of doubt and worry made everything sweeter, and Tanner was no exception. Brighton's immobile leg made things a challenge, but they were no less passionate. Tanner gently rolled him onto his stomach, and Brighton propped himself on his elbows and watched as Tanner stalked him from the bottom of the bed, licking his way up his good leg and then burying his lips and tongue between his legs. Brighton arched his back and howled like a banshee in heat. Tanner wrapped his arms around his hips and held him still, probing his opening until Brighton could barely see straight.

Once Brighton's brain had nearly shut down, Tanner shifted, careful not to put his weight on him. "I can't wait until I can make love to you face to face," Tanner whispered into his ear while Brighton panted to catch his breath.

"I know," he rasped in return. Tanner hugged Brighton around his chest, pressing them together. They kissed sloppily. Then Tanner made sure he was comfortable before rummaging in the drawer beside the bed. He found the lube, and Brighton closed his eyes, waiting as patiently as his thrumming body would allow. The rip of foil reached Brighton's ears, then after some fumbling, which he ignored, Tanner loomed over him. He felt Tanner's cock press for entrance.

They joined slowly and tenderly, Tanner filling his heart just as surely as he filled his body. Brighton gasped and whimpered softly. This was what he'd dreamed of those nights alone in the hospital. He hadn't let himself believe it could be real, that Tanner had actually picked him. But he had, and he was here—they were here together.

Tanner carefully shifted him to his side, and they moved together. There was no speed, no frantic coupling that shook the bed and rattled the beams. Instead it was quiet, tender, and caring. Every touch had special meaning. Brighton's small groans echoed and were picked up by Tanner only to be taken back again, added to, and then built on by Tanner once again, until the ultimate explosion left them both quiet, peaceful, and unable to move. Thankfully Brianne's trip to the store took longer than she'd anticipated.

CHAPTER 8

TANNER TRIED his best to calm Brighton down. If he hadn't been on crutches, he'd have paced a groove in the floor. "It's going to be all right," Tanner said with surprising clarity. Brighton's nerves were definitely getting to him.

"How do you know?" Brighton challenged.

A car crunched as it pulled into the drive. "Arthur is here." Thank goodness. Arthur was going to take Brighton to the hearing, and Tanner intended to follow as soon as he had the evening chores and feeding done.

"You'll be behind us, right?" Brighton asked.

"Yes. Don't worry. I won't be long." The hearing, on the other hand, could end up being very long. Arthur had warned them both that the process could be tedious. Tanner hugged Brighton to him, rubbing his back gently. "I'll be there with you, I promise." Tanner kissed him and then helped him out to the car. Once they had left, Tanner hurried to the barn and made sure all the animals were comfortable. The heat was hard on them this time of year. Tanner made sure they had plenty of water and opened the small windows to try to catch any evening breezes to help cool them.

When he was done, he went back to the house to change. He had just finished when Alicia and the boys arrived. One of the goats was particularly friendly when the boys came to visit. Tanner had gotten a collar and leash, and he guided the goat into a cage he'd borrowed from the farm supply store and carefully loaded it into the back of the truck.

"Are you sure you want to do this?" Alicia asked.

"Th… they don't think this is a real farm. So we'll show them," Tanner explained.

Alicia chuckled. "The zoning board isn't going to know what hit them."

"Let's hope so," Tanner said. He climbed into the truck and followed Alicia as she wound through the developments and past strip malls until they came to the more historic section of town. Tanner pulled into the parking lot next to the town hall. He opened the cage and attached the leash to the collar. Thankfully the goat didn't seem to mind it. Tanner lifted the goat into his arms.

"Follow Uncle Tanner," Alicia told the boys, and they walked right behind him. People paused curiously when they saw what Tanner had in his arms, but no one stopped him as he climbed the steps and entered the building. "I'll go see where they are. You two stay right here," she added to Marky and Josh, who both nodded. She walked away and returned a minute later. "They're just calling your case."

Tanner set the goat down and handed the leash to Marky. "Walk him gently down the hall. Your mom, Josh, and I will be with you. Once we open the d… door, Josh, you walk in with your brother." He grinned at the boys.

Alicia led them down the hall, and Tanner opened the door to the hearing room. He stood out of the way as Marky and Josh led the meandering goat down the aisle.

"Hi, Daddy," Josh called when he saw Arthur up front, sitting next to Brighton.

"Do you have an explanation for this?" an unfamiliar voice asked through the amplified sound system.

"The main question around this zoning change seems to be whether the property has been farmed and is still being used as a farm." Alicia entered and caught up to the boys, who had reached the front of the room to a chorus of soft awww's. She stood with them as Tanner entered the room, letting the door close behind him. Thankfully everyone was watching the goat as she looked around. "We can tell you that this is a farm, and we can show you pictures, but a demonstration has more impact. This is one of the goats that currently calls the farm home." Arthur seemed to be warming up to his theme. "There are others, along with sheep and a pony. All of which were there when Mr. McKenzie inherited the farm."

Josh let go of the leash and made a break for Arthur, but Alicia caught him and lifted him off his feet. Tanner stepped over and took him. Then he pointed to a row of chairs and except for the goat, they sat down.

"I'm sorry, but farm animals are not allowed in city hall," the man in the center of the panel, probably the chairman, said into the microphone.

"Actually, I checked, and there is nothing in any of the ordinances about livestock," Arthur said. "Pets are not allowed. But this goat is not a pet. It's on a leash to keep it under control, but it's livestock, a farm animal. So if I may continue?"

"All right." The chairman looked around. "We will stipulate that there is currently and has been livestock on the property." All the board members nodded their agreement.

"Then if you stipulate that, by extension, the land has been a farm and continues to be a working farm, and the request to change the zoning is based upon the assertion that the land hasn't been actively farmed in the last ten years, according to the letter that was sent to Mr. McKenzie. An assertion that is inaccurate based upon your own stipulation, which was just recorded."

Brighton was beginning to smile, and the members of the zoning board began shifting in their seats.

"But Mr. McKenzie is free to continue farming under the new zoning," the chairman said.

"True, but the basis for the change that was proposed no longer exists." Arthur turned to the zoning-board attorney, who sat on the other side of the room from the board.

"That's correct. This board does not have the authority to change zoning that is not properly requested. Since the assertion under which the zoning change was sought has been deemed to be false, you have no choice but to deny the zoning change."

The chairman looked at the others. "Let's take an official vote, then. Do I have a motion?"

"I move we deny the requested zoning change on the grounds that the request is invalid," a woman to the right of the chairman said.

"I second it," the man next to her added.

"All in favor?" the chairman asked, and everyone raised their hand. "Let the record show that the decision was unanimous and that the zoning change is denied." The chairman then turned to Arthur. "Could you please remove the goat from the hearing room in case it makes a mess?"

Alicia stood, and Marky led the goat out the back. Alicia followed him, and Tanner went as well, carrying Josh. He paused a second when he saw a woman glaring at him venomously. He figured she must be Brighton's aunt and shrugged before continuing on. Once they got outside, Tanner led Marky and the goat to the grass, which was getting a little long.

"That was a brilliant idea," Arthur said as he came to join them, helping Brighton navigate the stairs. "They couldn't argue with livestock in front of them."

"Will we need a zoning change to open the petting farm?" Brighton asked. "If we do, they might not be accommodating."

"Nope. The zoning as it is states agribusiness and what you want to do is just that. You're fine." Arthur smiled. The door to City Hall opened, and the scowling woman came out. Her expression hadn't changed. Brighton followed Tanner's gaze and sighed.

"You got what you wanted," she sniped.

"That's enough, Vera," the man behind her said forcefully. "That land is Brighton's, and he can do what he likes with it. Personally, I wish him well. He's already done more than your dad was able to do. He has plans for the place. It shows in what he's already done. And we have more than enough strip malls and condominiums already. Now let's go home. You've wasted enough time on this stupid bid to get your own way." He descended the stairs. "I've had it with this spoiled attitude. It's going to change, or I'll make some changes you won't like." Brighton's aunt followed behind him without making a sound.

Tanner turned away and saw Brighton do the same. He thought Brighton might have been trying not to laugh, but it was hard to tell.

"My God, I never expected him to stand up to her." Brighton turned to Arthur. "Thank you for everything." They shook hands, and then Brighton thanked the boys and Alicia. "You were great."

"Can we ride the pony when we get back?"

"How about you come over tomorrow, if it's okay with your mom. You can help feed the animals, and you can both ride the pony." That got jumps of excitement from Marky and nods from Josh. Alicia seemed pleased.

"Let's get these two home to bed," Arthur said as he took Josh from Tanner. They said their good-byes and left. Tanner led the goat to the truck and loaded her back into the cage. She settled right down, and then Tanner helped Brighton into the truck before walking around to the driver's side. He climbed in and shut the door but didn't start the engine.

"You won," Tanner whispered.

"I did." Brighton turned to him, biting his lower lip. "There will be a lot of work to do." He turned back and tilted his head down. It didn't take long for Tanner to figure out he was looking at his healing leg. "We'll need to develop detailed plans and lay out everything so there are no mistakes. Then we can arrange to get the buildings built and the additional livestock purchased."

Tanner started the engine and pulled out of the parking lot. "There will be lots of work. But we can do it." He drove back to the farm and pulled to a stop near the house. Tanner got out and carefully carried the goat back to the barn and put her in the pen. Then he sat on a bale of straw and watched as they all settled in for the night.

"Tanner, what are you doing?" Brighton asked as he came inside on his crutches.

"Just thinking."

"Me too," Brighton said. Tanner scooted over, and Brighton sat down next to him. "I've been thinking that I've liked having you here these past few days, and I want you to stay with me."

Tanner shifted his gaze. "But…?" he prompted. He'd heard the hesitation in Brighton's voice.

"I don't want you to think…."

"That it's just because of all the work there is to do?" Tanner asked.

Brighton nodded. "Yeah. I mean, you work here, and then we got involved, and now I love you, but I don't want you to think I'm taking advantage of you." Brighton huffed softly. "That's the last thing I want."

Tanner rolled his eyes. "I'm the quiet one, and you're the… worrywart." He reached over to Brighton and lightly squeezed his uninjured leg. "Do you want me to move in because of the work I do around here?"

"Of course not," Brighton answered. "I want you to move in because the house feels empty without you and the farm lifeless. I miss you when you aren't here. The bed seems so big when you aren't taking up most of it." He smiled. "But I like it because you hold me."

"I love you," Tanner whispered. He knew it was true. This felt so different from what he'd had with Royce. It was right and comfortable. "So yes, I'll move in here, but not right away. I still have my room at Arthur's, and I can keep it for a little while. Let's take it slow and see where things lead."

"So you'll have a backup plan," Brighton observed a little huffily.

"No. I'm saying we take it slow. I haven't exactly been spending many nights in my room since we met, but…." Tanner searched for the right words. "We've only known each other a few weeks. Things got very rushed with Royce, and then they went to hell…."

"Okay," Brighton said. "I think I understand, and not rushing into things is probably a good idea."

Tanner put his arm around Brighton's shoulders and shifted slightly until Brighton leaned against him. "It's peaceful here." He closed his eyes. He knew he wasn't in Montana, too many cars went by on the street out front, but in the barn, with the shuffle of the animals in their pens and the occasional bleat or baa, it was peaceful and safe. Life could go at a slower pace than it did just a short distance away.

"Who would have thought we could have our own little piece of the country in the middle of the city?" Brighton asked. Tanner hummed his answer and held Brighton a little tighter. They sat for a while, just thinking, as darkness descended. The last of the light coming in the windows was about to fade when Tanner stood and lifted Brighton into his arms.

"I can go back on my own," Brighton said, holding on to his crutches.

Tanner nodded and carried him out of the barn. He secured the door and then strode across the yard and into the house. He stopped long enough to kick the door open and then climbed the stairs. Tanner waited for Brighton to open the bedroom door, and then they were inside. He put Brighton down on the bed, set the crutches aside, and began undressing him.

"I thought we were taking our time...." Brighton chuckled as Tanner nearly ripped his shirt getting it off.

"We can go slow... later." Tanner got Brighton's pants and shoes off and then started on his own clothes.

"I can live with that," Brighton said, and Tanner kissed him. That was more than enough talking for a while... shouting, moaning, and the occasional scream, yes, but talking? No.

EPILOGUE

"I LOVE spring." Tanner heard the woman say as he finished up with the sheep. "All the babies." He lifted one of the lambs and stepped toward the edge of their pen, where a group of school kids, their teacher, and chaperones waited.

"This is Peep," Tanner said. He was still nervous talking in front of people, but kids never bothered him. They were so open and always so excited to hear what he had to say. "He's eight weeks old."

"Can I hold him?" one of the kids in the class asked.

"No, but you can each pet him as long as you're gentle," Tanner said, and the kids lined up quickly. They approached one by one, and Tanner let them pet Peep, who soaked in the attention.

"He's really soft," one of the kids said as he took his turn. Once everyone had had a chance to stroke Peep's back, he set him down, and the lamb raced around the pen before hurrying back to his mother. The woman was right—Tanner loved spring too, and this was turning into a very special one.

"We're going to see the goats now, and then we'll break into groups, and you can have a few minutes to look around."

The original plan had been to have the goats and sheep in the existing barn, but after the addition of a few sheep, one of which turned out to be pregnant, their little flock grew quickly, so they put an addition onto the original barn with its own entrance and completely separate area. It had worked out perfectly. Tanner followed the class to the goat area and gave his little talk about goats, their milk, and how they cared for them. He let them look into the enclosure where they kept the babies, but the mothers weren't going to allow any of their young to be handled. The babies were too young and the mothers too protective at the moment. "If you go up to the enclosure, you can feed them."

He and Brighton had put in a gumball-type machine that dispensed feed for a quarter. It helped pay for the feed, and they made sure a good amount was dispensed each time. Tanner left the barn as the kids fanned out into groups. Alicia was busy over at the pony rides. When they opened a few weeks ago, she had said she wanted some time out of the house, and since she used to ride when she was a teenager, she worked the pony ride on Saturday and Sunday afternoons and on days like today, when they had a school class visiting.

"It's going well," Brighton said as he walked up to Tanner.

"It is. The teacher said she was very impressed with how things looked and would recommend us to other schools." His stutter faded much of the time. Tanner noticed it reappeared only when he was nervous or unsure of himself. "I think we need to consider some walking paths back through the orchard and the pumpkin patch. The kids can walk through the old orchard and then into the new plantings. It will also allow us to control the flow through the patch this fall, when the pumpkins start to ripen."

They had done so much already—built animal housing, added paths, and planted grass alongside the paths. They had put in flowers to make the place look appealing. The pumpkin patch had been tilled and planted. The orchard had come back strong, and the new trees were growing well. There was still a section of the land that they hadn't decided what they wanted to do with, but they had time, and first they needed to see what worked and what didn't. So far, the animals worked—the kids loved them, judging by the laughter and delighted screams that echoed across the farm.

"I think we need to add pigs and a few cows," Brighton said.

"I think so too. The smaller animals are good, but the kids keep asking what else they can pet. I was also thinking a few chickens. The teacher asked for those." Tanner hated chickens. Every time he was around them the damn things pecked him to death. "We might think about adding a turkey as well."

"All right. Let's check out the cost of adding an aviary to the property," Brighton agreed. "Now that we have money coming in, we can look at some other things."

"So it's doing okay?"

Brighton nodded. "We expected it to be slow to start, but we've been busy, and it's getting busier. I also got a call this morning from a guy who lives out in Frederick. He does salvage, and he happened on some fairy-tale characters from an old amusement park. He has Little Bo Peep, Johnny Appleseed, Jack and the Beanstalk, Simple Simon, Red Riding Hood, and Little Miss Muffet. He says they're in good shape. He's got some other things as well and is going to be passing through on his way back home to Frederick, so I told him to stop by. They're very affordable, and we could put the figures throughout the farm. I think it would add to the fun for the kids, and they're what it's all about."

A car pulled in, and Brighton headed off to the front to greet the new customers. For now they had foregone a ticket booth in favor of a more personal greeting, but that would probably need to change soon. Tanner stood back and watched Brighton do his thing. He walked so easily now. Brighton had been able to help with a lot of the manual labor their new business required, and when things got to be too much… well, they had a routine that included massage and lots of touching. Tanner was all about the touching. Watching Brighton, Tanner expected him to do his meet-and-greet with the guests, but a familiar woman got out of the car.

"Aunt Vera," Brighton said, and Tanner instantly tensed. That woman had been a pain in Brighton's behind ever since the zoning board hearing. "What do you want?"

He didn't hear her answer, but Brighton returned to where Tanner stood near the entrance with his aunt following him. "I wanted to see how the animals were being treated," she said.

Tanner turned around. "You can leave," he told her firmly.

"I have a right—"

Tanner cut her off. "You have no rights here. This is Brighton's farm, not yours." Tanner turned to Brighton. The woman had shown up at the oddest times and had nearly lost them a contractor when she had stuck her nose into things that were none of her business.

"Do I need to get a restraining order?" Brighton asked. "You have no say here. This is our farm, and we are carrying on what Grandpa wanted. He might not have envisioned this, but he would love that children are visiting his farm and having a great time. So what's the problem? If this is still about the will, you can give it up. Tanner and I have built something here, and we're going to work to see it grow. You need to accept that."

"This was where I grew up, and now it's—"

Brighton gaped at her. "You were the one who wanted to sell the farm in the first place, and now that it looks different but it's still here, you're upset." Brighton took a step back and shook his head. "I think you should go home now, and it'd be best if you don't come back. This is our home, mine and Tanner's. It's our farm. We'll fight to protect it and to protect our privacy and our lives together." Brighton stepped closer to him. "He's what's important. I don't really know what's going on in that head of yours, but we've had enough. My next call will be to my lawyer, and then a restraining order will be filed. I hope you understand that." Brighton kept his voice low and his tone surprisingly light despite the message he was delivering. "So please leave now."

"But we…," she sputtered.

"Whatever you did for Brianne and me has long been used up. She's happy, and I'm happy here with Tanner. I suggest you find what will make you happy, but whatever it is, it isn't and can't be here." Brighton stared her down until she turned and walked back to her car.

"I know that was hard," Tanner said.

"I don't understand why she has to act like everyone owes her something." Tanner stood next to Brighton as she turned her car around and drove away. "We built this together, you and me, and I'm proud of it. She still thinks that part of this is hers, but it's not. She didn't spend days laying sod or hauling mulch to make the paths. She didn't spend cold nights making sure the animals—our animals—were warm enough. You and I did that, and we care for the animals each and every day."

"Brighton," Tanner began.

"This is our farm and our business, and she can keep her old biddy nose out of it."

"Our farm?" Tanner asked.

"Of course. Our farm." Brighton turned to him. "You moved in with me, and you've shared my life for months. You worked right alongside me to help build buildings... hell, you've done more than I have. So of course this is our farm, and when we're ready and this whole inheritance thing is settled, we'll go down to the county offices in Columbia, purchase a marriage license, and then it will legally be *our* farm."

Tanner was shocked. Somehow he hadn't expected Brighton to feel this way, or at least they hadn't talked about this before. Of course, the past few months had been so busy they hadn't had a chance to talk about a great deal other than the farm, and at night when they were alone, they didn't talk much, which was as it should be as far as Tanner was concerned.

"So did you just ask me to m... marry you?" The stutter was back.

"Yes, I think I did. I could get down on one knee if you like." Brighton smiled, and Tanner wanted to take him into his arms, but they were outside with guests, and that required a sense of decorum.

Tanner tilted his head toward the house, and they stepped up onto the porch and then just inside the front door. "Yes," Tanner said and then pulled Brighton into his arms. "I'll marry you and spend the rest of my life with you, here on this farm."

"I always wondered if you missed the open land," Brighton said.

"What we have here is land enough." Tanner let his lips do the talking, and not with words. Once Brighton pressed against him and could barely stand, Tanner backed away and took his hand. They had a farm to run and guests to see to. They would celebrate their promises tonight when the farm was quiet and it was only them.

"I love you," Brighton whispered.

"I love you too," Tanner said, cupping Brighton's cheek in his hand. He kissed Brighton one more time and then opened the door, and together they stepped out into the spring sunshine.

ANDREW GREY grew up in western Michigan with a father who loved to tell stories and a mother who loved to read them. Since then he has lived all over the country and traveled throughout the world. He has a master's degree from the University of Wisconsin-Milwaukee and now works full time on his writing. Andrew's hobbies include collecting antiques, gardening, and leaving his dirty dishes anywhere but in the sink (particularly when writing). He considers himself blessed with an accepting family, fantastic friends, and the world's most supportive and loving husband. Andrew currently lives in beautiful historic Carlisle, Pennsylvania.

Visit Andrew's website at http://www.andrewgreybooks.com and blog at http://andrewgreybooks.livejournal.com/.

E-mail him at andrewgrey@comcast.net.

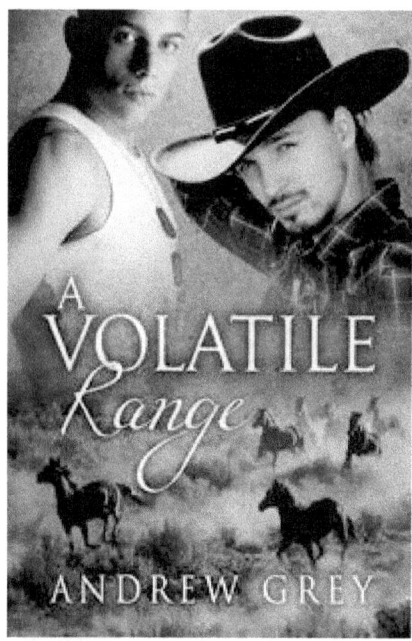

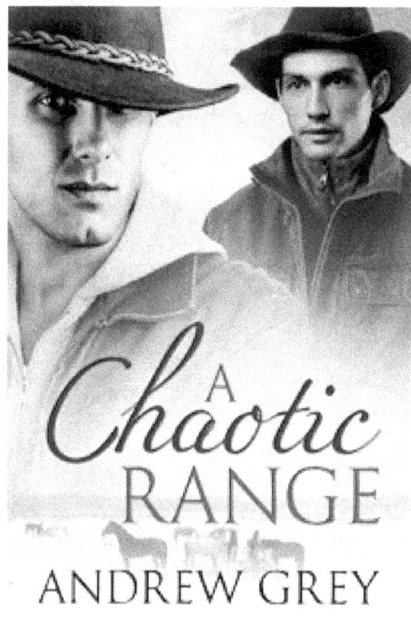

http://www.dreamspinnerpress.com

A
COURAGEOUS
RIDE

ANDREW
GREY

FIRE AND
Water

ANDREW GREY

THE
FIGHT
WITHIN

ANDREW GREY

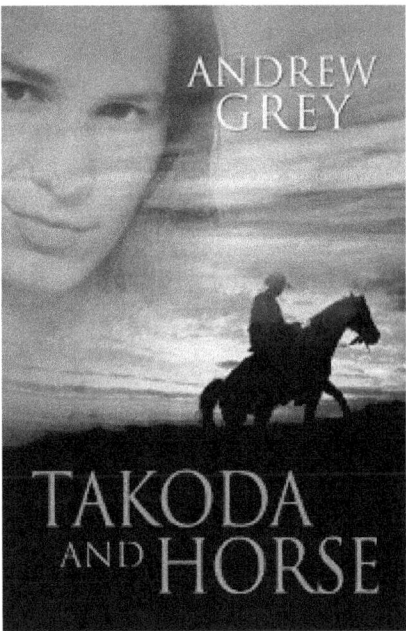

ANDREW
GREY

TAKODA
AND HORSE

http://www.dreamspinnerpress.com

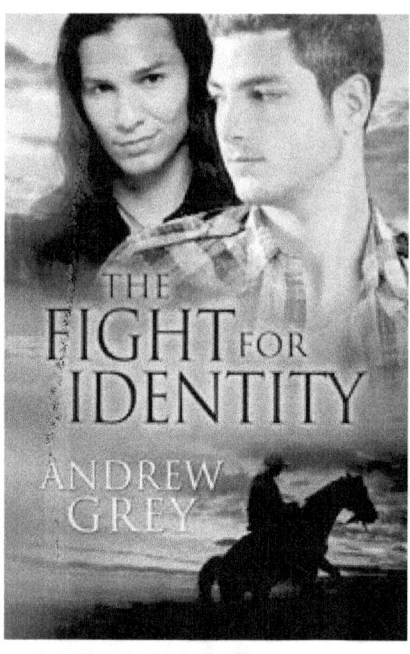

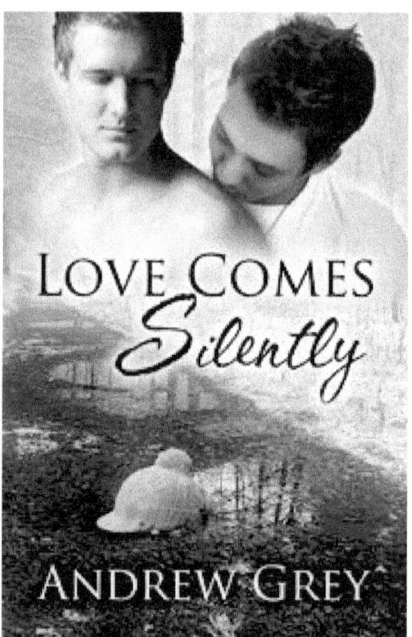

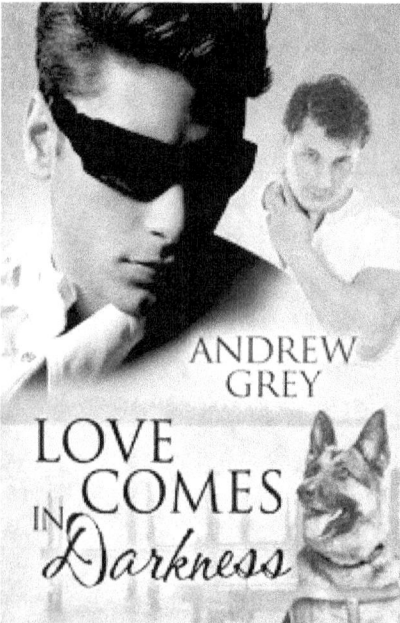

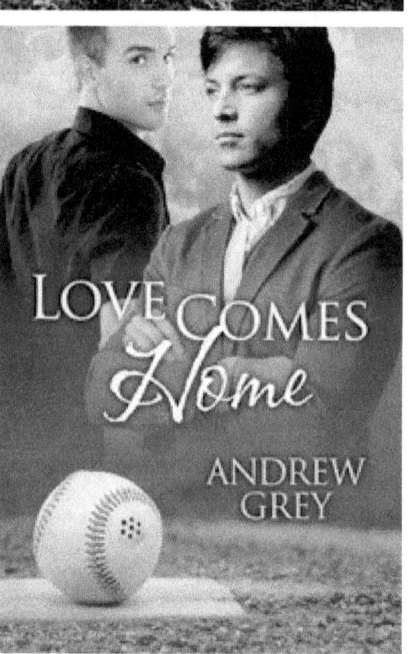

http://www.dreamspinnerpress.com

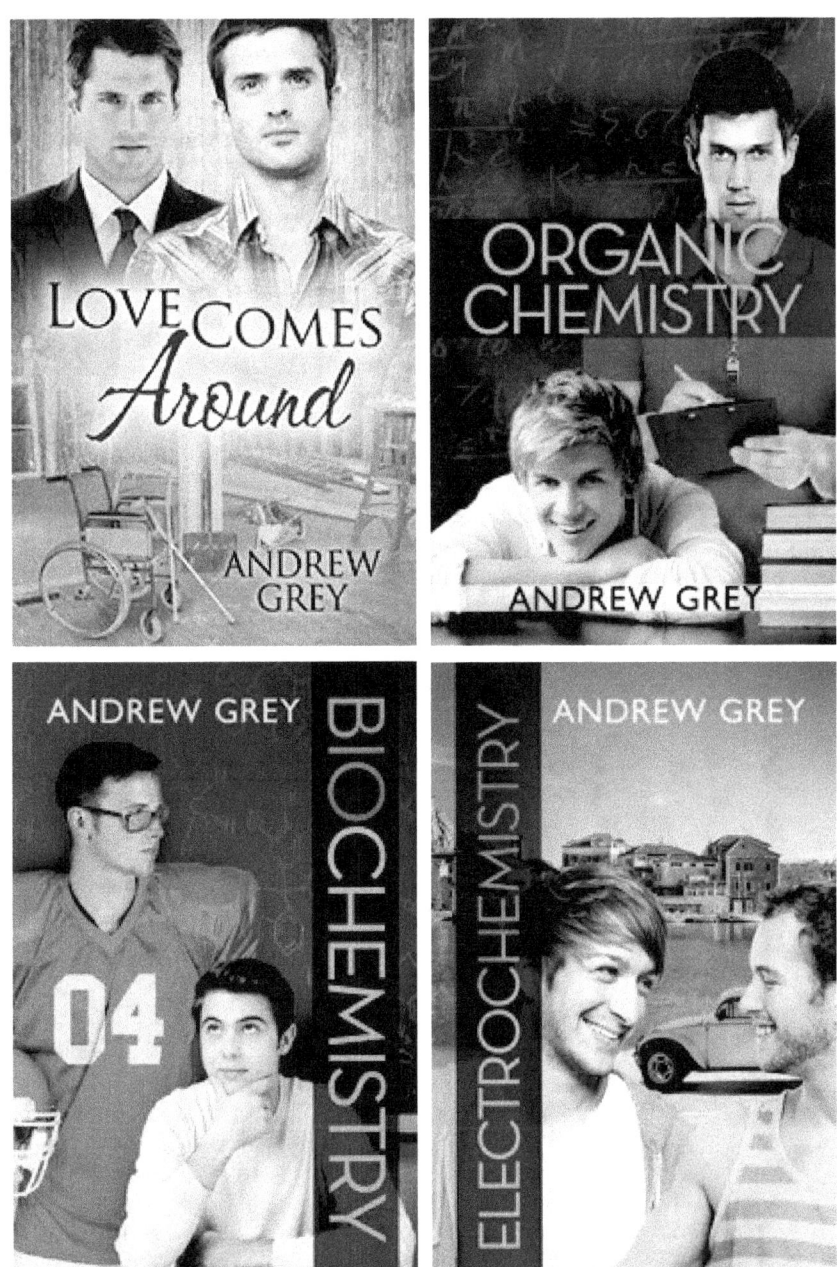

http://www.dreamspinnerpress.com

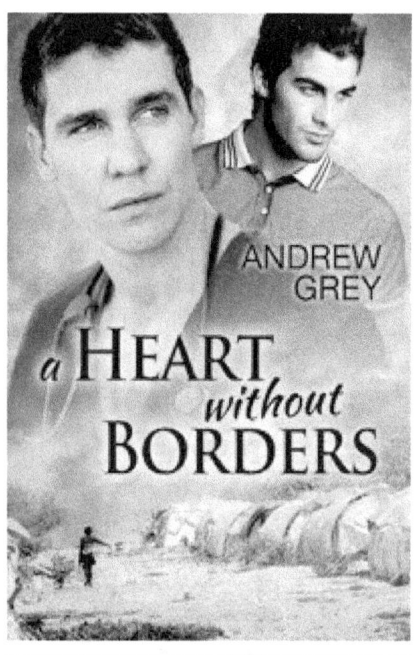

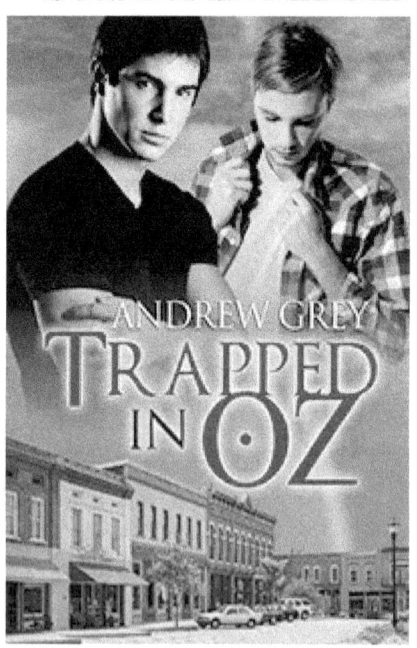

http://www.dreamspinnerpress.com

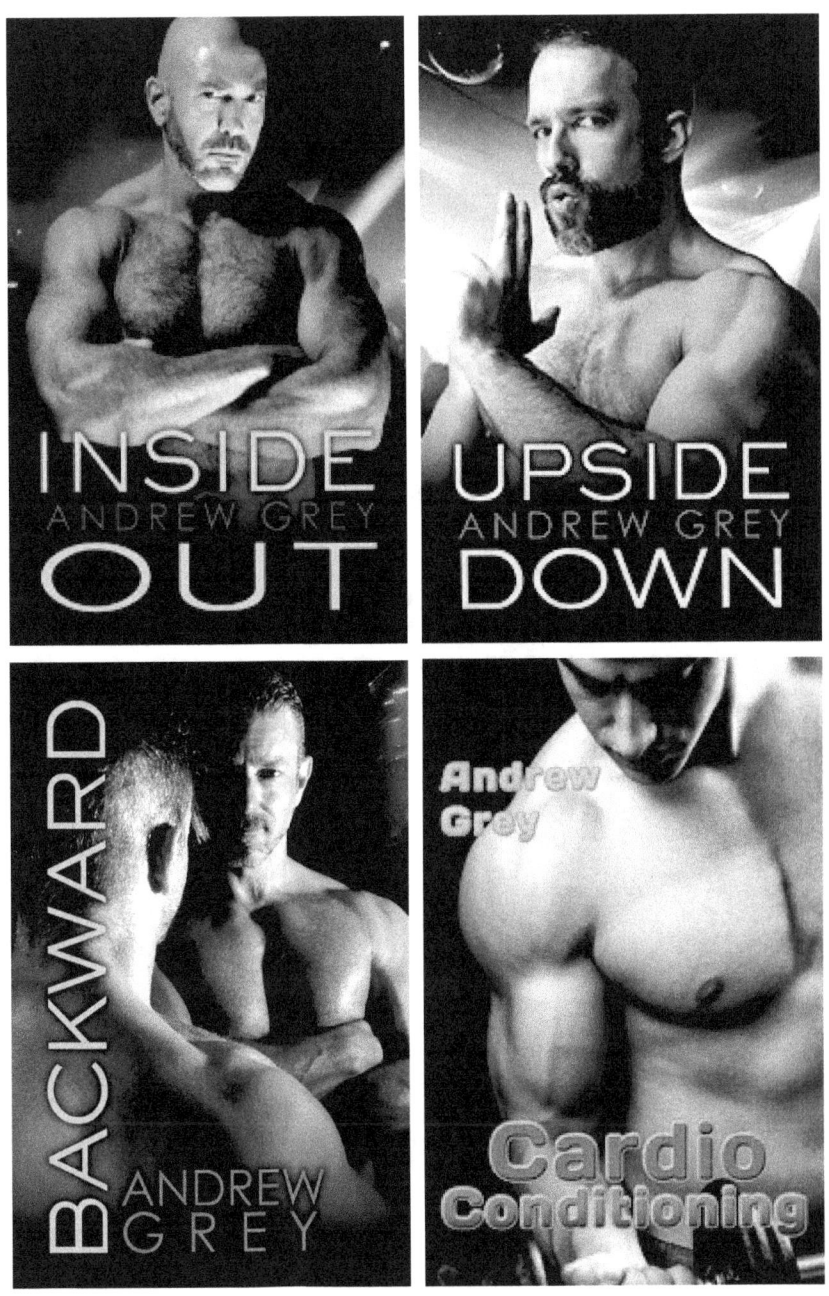

http://www.dreamspinnerpress.com

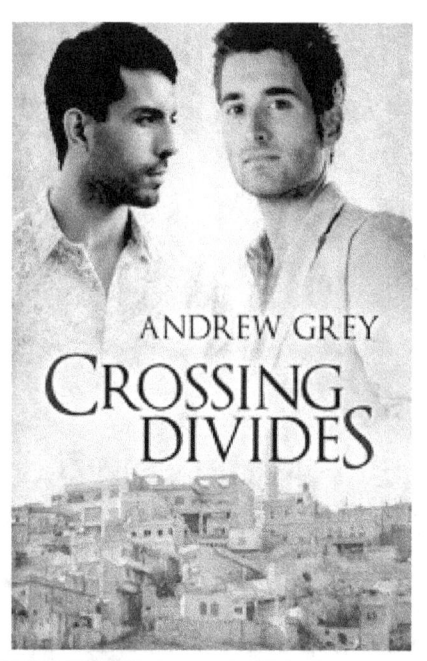

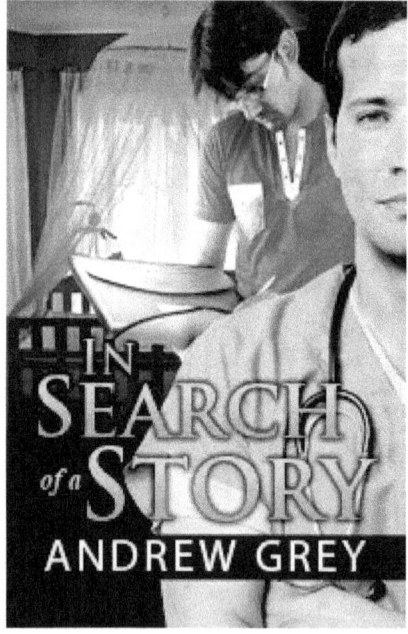

http://www.dreamspinnerpress.com

http://www.dreamspinnerpress.com

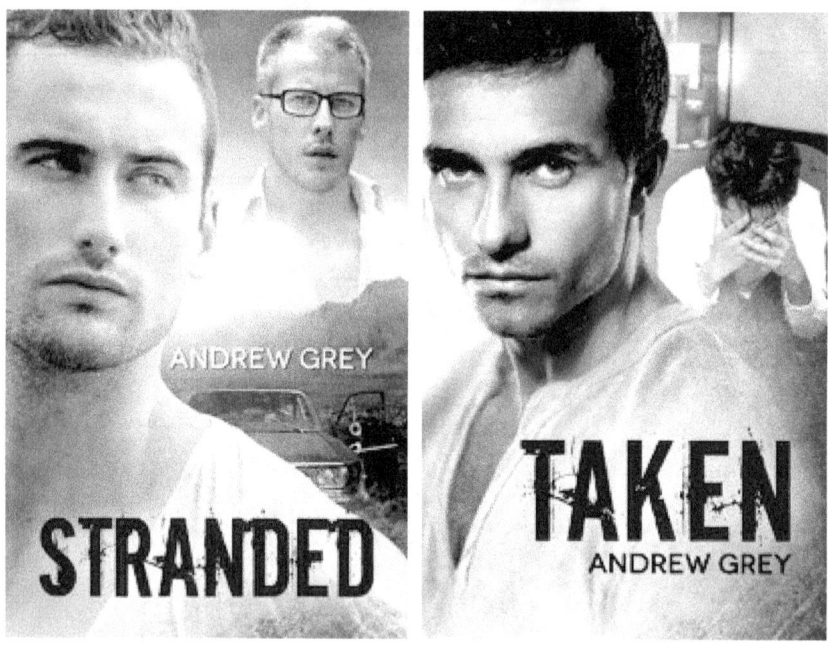

http://www.dreamspinnerpress.com

http://www.dreamspinnerpress.com

FOR **MORE** OF THE **BEST GAY ROMANCE**

DREAMSPINNER
PRESS
dreamspinnerpress.com